CITY OF SPELLS

A HAUNTED FLORIDA NOVEL

GABY TRIANA

ISBN: 9781731100221 (Paperback Edition)
ASIN: B07HFKCY3J (eBook Edition)

Characters and events in this book are fictitious. Any similarity to real persons, living or dead, is coincidental and not intended by the author.

Book cover and interior design by Curtis Sponsler

Printed and bound in the United States of America
First printing November 2018

Published by Alienhead Press
Miami, FL 33186

Visit Gaby Triana at www.gabytriana.com

ONE

1921
Prohibition

Julia Harding stared at the bay, waiting for a man who was not her husband. She cradled her small belly, thankful that the housekeeper had not yet begun asking questions.

The Siren was late, and her nerves were shot.

Her husband, Peter Wallace Harding, New York City millionaire, had been hired by railroad tycoon, Henry Flagler, to oversee construction of a new hotel—the Palm Oasis—in West Palm Beach. Problem was, he'd been there the last year and a half. His last trip home had been two months ago and only for one day. When he'd next arrive—*if* he'd arrive at all, for his activities had grown more and more lawless as of late—he would come by Flagler's new train.

Originally, Mr. Harding wasn't supposed to supervise construction of the Palm Oasis in West Palm Beach. He'd been hired to oversee the Flamingo Hotel in Miami Beach, a much-shorter twenty miles from their newly-built home. Else Julia never would have agreed to settle here. But Mr. Harding had insisted all these new hotels would make even more money for them, and so she'd agreed.

Now, she regretted doing so, for Julia felt forsaken. Discarded like a cancelled stamp. Left to live out lonely days by the sea with no one other than her Bahamian housekeeper to talk to, and Mimi could be so…*insightful*, it scared Julia.

Whenever Mimi would stroll into the room carrying fresh linens, she'd catch Julia standing at the lavatory, pressing a towel to her flushed face. Every morning, Julia would rush upstairs and empty the contents of her stomach into the water closet in a futile attempt to keep breakfast down.

She knows, Julia thought.

Still, it could be her husband's.

No one would know until June the following year. And then, the moment of truth would come. For her husband had been home the same week as Roger Gibson's delivery, and Roger Gibson, like Mimi, possessed dark and lovely Bahamian features.

It should've been a charmed existence, living in this mansion by Cayo de Biscainhos, a gleaming azure body of water dazzling with diamonds in the sunlight. Her husband had convinced her that moving to freeze-proof Miami, a world away from frigid New York, would be a magnificent opportunity. He could take advantage of the booming land development business. He could take advantage of Mr. Flagler's superior wages.

Best of all, he could take advantage of the lack of law enforcement in South Florida. For this reason, many men had migrated south. It was harder to be arrested in No Man's Land, easier to deal with smugglers, and the proximity to the Caribbean islands where rum was produced at a frantic rate made Miami's coastline a bootlegger's dream come true.

Except that Julia had been left to fend for herself, and she knew her onions. She knew what her husband kept hidden in the subterranean cellar behind the false façade

2

and 300-lb vault door, surrounded by walls of limestone and crushed shells. Four hundred cases, maybe more, of illegal spirits.

How could Mr. Harding leave her to protect such a thing without so much as a single weapon?

And so every day, she watched the vessels in the bay, hoping one would be Roger in *The Siren* come to visit and deliver more cases. She allowed herself to fantasize that one day, Roger might take her away from this lackluster life, love her, give her what her heart had always wanted—attention. Roger was the only man who kept her sane, the only one who cared about Julia, but unfortunately, he was also the man with whom she could never be.

With a repressed sob, she turned back to the house and found Mimi coming up the walk.

"Mrs. Harding," Mimi said, out of breath. "A man called on the telephone. He said to tell you that your husband would be home soon."

"What do we call soon today?"

"A month's time."

"A month?" Julia exclaimed.

She would be showing by then, if her body survived it, and sometimes she wondered if it would be better to lose the child. God only knew the consequences that might befall her if he or she did not resemble her husband come June?

God also knew how much she had always wanted a child to keep her busy during these long days and nights. But she had never expected to be dumped in this forsaken tropical hell, as beautiful as it was. She had never expected to feel so lonely, to stray like another man's Sheba. But it was her husband's custom to always dump her somewhere. In New York, it was at the Ladies'

Empire Club, or the Tea Room, as long as it allowed him to conduct his business without interference.

Her life meant nothing to him.

"Sure, tell it to Sweeney," Julia said with a sigh. A month would become three, or four, or never. "Please get supper started. The men are not coming today."

The sun was already setting, and if deliveries were to be made, she would have spied them on the horizon by now. Julia turned her back to the bay and headed to the house, Mimi following close behind, when the faint sound of a motor reached Julia's ears.

She turned.

Her heart lifted, but only for a moment.

From the vessel's silhouettes, it was not Roger nor one of his rum runners stopping by to check on her. Lead plummeted into her stomach.

"Go inside, please," Julia told Mimi.

"Yes, ma'am."

She turned and waited for the Coast Guard to come closer, so she could assess its intentions. It did not appear to be passing through—it was stopping. Julia braced herself. Moments like these made her resent Mr. Harding the most.

When the boat finally docked, out stepped the captain, a handsome, older man. "Good evening, missus. Is your husband home?" he asked, lighting a cigar.

"No, he's a land developer doing business in West Palm. Is everything to order?"

"Not exactly. We're intercepting boats from Bimini and Gun Cay along the Rum Line. Some have been seen headed for these coasts. You wouldn't happen to have seen any stopping here, would you?"

Julia swallowed her dread as quietly as she could. "Of course not. Why are they being intercepted?" she asked, hoping she sounded innocent.

The captain looked at Julia through eyes that had seen too much. "Nothing to concern yourself with, missus, but if you'll excuse me, I'll need to inspect your property."

"For?"

Nerves jittered inside her stomach. Had she sounded too brusque just then?

The Coast Guard had stopped once before to ask questions but never to inspect the house. Mr. Harding shouldn't have gotten involved with the trade. She'd never voiced her concern, though, as it had not been her place.

"Again, matters you needn't worry yourself with. Won't you show me in?" He tipped his hat politely.

Julia felt trapped. "Yes, of course."

She had no choice. If she appeared the least bit resistant, it would mark her as guilty, or suspicious at the very least. Like her husband had coached her before he left: *Anyone shows up, show them around, be pleasant, offer coffee or tea.* She never thought they would actually stop in— after all, this was the beauty of living close to the islands—but news around town was that law enforcement was beginning to catch on.

The captain, along with two other men, stepped out of the boat and followed her down the unlit path to the house. Julia eyed the banyan tree in her garden and wondered if she would ever sit beneath it again.

Their cellar was filled to the brim with illegal spirits, but if she was lucky, it'd be difficult to find. They would have to stay a while, probe, raid the home.

Julia showed the men into her house. "May I offer you some coffee, tea, perhaps some fresh water?"

"You sure those are all the choices?" The captain chuckled under his breath. He strolled the house, tapping on walls, peeking behind framed art.

Julia did not reply.

Normally, she would turn on her charming self, but as of late, she was not feeling much like a hostess. It could've been her delicate state, or the fact that Roger had not visited this week, or perhaps it was the enormous lie that was her entire life weighing heavily on her.

"Water would be fine," the man replied.

Julia glanced at Mimi who nodded and set to serving the Coast Guard captain a glass of water. She wondered if there existed some way to inquire about the captured speedboat without incriminating herself.

"The, uh…speedboats you intercepted. Were they Bahamian vessels?"

The captain raised an eyebrow, as Mimi brought the glass of water then disappeared down the hall. "Why the interest in Bahamian vessels, missus?" the captain asked.

Julia touched her collarbone. "Why, I'm simply wondering where the rum is coming from. Making small talk." She forced a smile.

"It comes from all over the region, Mrs…"

"Harding."

"Mrs. Harding. And not just rum but whiskey, wine, all sorts of booze. The ship we intercepted this morning was from Nassau."

"Nassau?"

Roger was from Nassau. Julia tried to keep a steady expression.

Mimi emerged from the hallway leading to the door underneath the carpet, the one that dropped into the cellar. She gave Julia a knowing look, and Julia knew she had gone like a good girl to double check on the latches.

The men lingered near the hallway.

Seeing the housekeeper emerge from there, one officer slowly stepped down the hallway, checking behind the large Egyptian tapestry Mr. Harding had purchased from John Rockefeller in Manhattan.

The captain kept one eye on his men and another on Julia. "The details are apt to frighten a young woman such as yourself, Mrs. Harding. I'd rather not say."

"Oh, you'd be surprised, Captain. Not much goes on around here. I'd be grateful to hear a tale or two." Yes, that sounded sincere.

"Very well, then." He took a long chug of his drink before wiping his mouth with the back of his hand. Roger did the same whenever he'd come in from spending days at sea.

"Captain McCoy is out there. And he's a smart one, you see. Brings spirits from all over the Caribbean to just outside that three-mile international line. Then, he lets smaller boats take over, face the danger of getting intercepted. We've caught onto his strategy."

"I see." Julia tried to seem interested, but inside, her chest imploded with anguish.

"These boats, some of them fitted with plane engines from the Great War, are faster than we are, Mrs. Harding. And the captains of these boats, some of them make several hundred-thousand dollars a year. I make *six* thousand for abiding the law. Do you think that's fair, Mrs. Harding?"

"Oh, definitely not."

"Definitely not." He puffed on his cigar.

Roger's boat was one of the ones fitted with a plane engine. He had talked incessantly about it last time he'd visited, he'd been so proud.

The captain stepped closer. Deep blue eyes burned with something unreadable.

"So, when we see these boats creeping up to homes like yours behind their smoke screens in the middle of the night, Mrs. Harding, I get a feeling deep inside my gut. You understand, don't you?"

Julia did not answer. He wanted her to incriminate herself, to say something—anything—but she would not.

If she had just *one* thing to live for, it was seeing Roger Gibson again. If these men discovered the contents of their secret room, and if the rum runners captured this morning included Roger, her life would be over.

The captain laughed then handed her back the empty glass. "Thank you. For the water." He winked at her.

He knew.

Through her moment of silence, she'd told him everything he needed to know.

Suddenly, one of his men walked into the house from the dock, waving a cracked bottle of rum in the air. "Captain, found this under the dock along with a few others."

Damn it, she and Mimi had cleaned the shore as best as they could, but these bottles washed up all the time.

The captain gave Julia a burning glare. "Raid the house," he ordered.

"No," Julia said. "Please."

He ignored her and headed straight for the secret door, as men bustled all around her.

Mimi's terrified stare met hers.

"Run," Julia told her. "Go out the front door and run as fast as you can. Do not look back."

"Yes, ma'am." The young woman dropped her apron and ran from the house away from the hubbub while Julia thought of what to do for herself.

Minutes blurred together, as she helplessly watched the raid on her home. Men ran everywhere, bullets sounded from deep inside the house, and she could imagine the vault door getting torn apart. Door by door, tapestry by tapestry, floorboard by floorboard, they ripped apart her home.

But it had never really been home, had it?

Julia stood by, too panicked to move.

"Oh, and Mrs. Harding?" The captain calmly puffed on his cigar. He paused at the top of the cellar stairs. "*The Siren's* captain opened fire on us this morning. We had no choice but to shoot him. You can tell your husband his rum runner is dead."

He disappeared into the cellar, taking Julia's heart with him.

No, it can't be.

Julia backed out of the house, as chaos erupted all around her. Men yelled to each other, brought out cases, cracked them open, confirmed the smuggled goods. Yelps of victory signaled her demise.

He'll never stop to see me again.
He'll never take me away from this life.
Or see his child.

As in a slow-moving dream, Julia floated toward her garden and stood perfectly still, staring up at the great banyan tree. It had given her hours of comfort during her year and a half of solitude. Cradling her belly, she thought of Roger, of the life they would never have, the one she'd dared to dream could ever be reality.

Dreams that had kept her sane.

Kept her alive.

Now with Roger gone, so had all hope.

Removing her shoes, she climbed the tree as she'd done many times before. Soon, Mr. Harding would be arrested. Their mansion would be sold, and new residents would eventually move in. Slipping one of the hundreds of hanging vines around her neck, tying it tightly, Julia muttered a curse.

As long as this house stood, facing the bay like a woman awaiting her lover's return, she could not allow another to experience the happiness that should have rightfully been hers. No love, no children, no family.

Closing her eyes, Julia dropped from the banyan's great branch, freeing herself from misery forever.

TWO

Present Day

The lucky knot bracelet around my wrist felt tighter than usual. I loosened it, remembering the day I got it. It was last year when Samuel and I visited the Buddhist temple in Miami Beach. The monk who'd put it on me had recited several mantras, infusing the bracelet with positive energy. He'd told me that when it was time, I should pass it onto someone else. Passing good energy was good karma.

It would bring me a world of luck in no time.

Good, because I need luck, I remembered thinking.

As a general rule, I tried not to think of things I *needed*. The more we put desires up on a pedestal, the more unattainable they seemed. Instead, I tried thinking of my desires as things I already *had* or were on their way. Like stuff I'd ordered on Amazon Prime, *God-Universe Edition*.

Well, my luck hadn't arrived in two days after that temple visit like Prime Shipping. But a year later, here I was inside my brand new shop—my dream come true.

It might've been the bracelet.

Or the Universe having heard my prayer.

But most likely, it'd been my own hard work.

Nestled on a side street off a main shopping plaza in Coconut Grove, *Goddess Moon* was now officially open for business. My little new age shop was filled with beautiful spiritual items, everything from crystals to incense, to religious statues, to yoga clothes, books on every metaphysical topic, but more importantly—wonderful people.

I'd assembled a team of three talented women and one sweet, non-binary lovely, Rain, who stood by ready to offer awesome services, such as aura photography, tarot readings, yoga classes, reiki energy healing, past-life hypnotherapy, and much more.

But only Bibi, Maggie, and I were on the schedule for today. Lorena, my reiki master, and Rain, my aura photographer, would be in tomorrow.

At twenty, Bibi was already a talented intuitive. She'd told me things about myself nobody could possibly know. She'd been doing so since the days when I used to babysit her. Maggie, older than me at forty, was an amazing hypnotherapist. According to her cards, I'd been a politician, a gravedigger, and a hippie in another life. The hippie I could see, but a gravedigger?

Really?

I'd hoped she'd tell me I'd been a psychic, a healing woman, a shaman, or some other kind of *bruja*. All my life, I'd identified as a witchy woman, minus the talent. This was why I'd hired such amazing people for my shop.

Because I envied them.

I didn't go around admitting this to my psychic friends, but I wasn't one of them. As much as I tried, I couldn't see ghosts, couldn't speak with spirit guides, couldn't see colorful auras, no matter how much I stared at people against a white background.

I meditated every day, sometimes twice. I tried tips and tricks from every religion to reach that prized alpha state, but I hated to say it—I was just...normal. My worries about bills, thoughts about whether my husband was happy, whether or not we'd ever be blessed with children, what I should make for dinner that evening always ruined my sessions. Never did I receive messages from my higher self.

Spirit guides did not visit me. Portals to the universe did not open up in my third eye. Candles did not flicker around me when the presence of a spirit was near.

Zero.

Nada.

As my Cuban parents would say, *No arrugue que no hay quien planche.* In other words, *Stop making waves, Queylin, you're just like everybody else.*

Still, with or without the world's encouragement, I would keep trying.

My spiritual journey began three years ago when Samuel and I went to Sedona for our honeymoon. I didn't know it at the time, but something about the vortexes there (not vortices) awakened a pursuit inside of me.

We came home, and this thirty-year-old Catholic girl launched on a mission for answers. I studied it all—Hinduism, Buddhism, Judaism, Santería, Haitian Vodou, pagan witchcraft, you name it. Miami was perfect for this, because its millions of residents cast their wishes into the Universe a million different ways.

A city of spells.

Maybe *Goddess Moon* was my way of being special, of showing commitment. If I hung around psychics long enough, I was bound to become one, right?

In the meantime, I tried not giving the sad, sympathetic looks from my psychic friends who knew I was born a "Muggle" any energy. I tried to ignore their gripes about how having been born with a sixth sense was *soo* annoying. After all, here I was wishing I could have one.

So, this bracelet gave me hope. If my dream store finally opened, maybe that elusive third eye would blast right open too.

I'd just finished lighting my seventh Nag Champa incense stick of the day and was rearranging the essential oils Bibi had put in alphabetical order (I preferred to have them grouped by desire the oil would attract—love, money, sex...) when the store bell rang ten minutes before closing.

"Welcome to *Goddess Moon*," I chirped.

"Hello!" Bibi added by her spot by the Tibetan singing bowls.

Only a handful of customers had come through today, one to buy a tumbled quartz crystal, one to buy a Tree of Life pendant, and a woman who couldn't decide on anything, so I was happy to wait on more. So far, the store hadn't begun turning a profit.

I turned to see an older gentleman with white hair and a sun-weathered face. He was fit for an older man and wore an almond *guayabera* with the requisite cigar in the pocket, the standard uniform of my grandparents' generation.

"*Buenas*," he said in Cuban Spanish.

"*Buenas*," I replied.

My Spanish was okay. I was a second generation American. My parents had come to Miami from Cuba in the 1970s. They spoke perfect English by the time they had me, so I was raised speaking both languages in the home. My mother called it "kitchen Spanish," the kind used in casual conversations. It was the best I could do.

"Can I help you find something?" Bibi asked.

Bibi was young and pretty, and this man, coming from a different time, place, and sense of *machismo*, stared at her body unabashedly as he walked past. Bibi breathed in deeply and returned to a sketch she was working on in a Moleskine journal. I didn't need to be psychic to feel her annoyance halfway across the room.

Ripping his gaze away from Bibi, he touched the table displaying crystal spheres to balance himself. He seemed exhausted, mentally or physically, I wasn't sure. Removing his glasses, wiping them on a tissue he pulled from his pocket, he spoke with soft command.

"I need someone adept in the spiritual arts," the gentleman said in his heavy accent.

"By spiritual arts, you mean…" I walked toward him with a smile.

He placed his glasses back on his nose, the tissue back in his pocket, and he looked at me. "Someone who can speak with ghosts."

"Ah."

I immediately thought of Lorena. But also Maggie. And Rain. Hell, Bibi could probably qualify as well, but I knew she didn't like doing house calls, and it seemed this man wanted just that.

"You don't have someone who can speak with ghosts?" he asked after my moment of silence.

"I do. We do, actually. But what, specifically, do you need?" I asked.

"I need someone to come to my home. To rid the house of unwanted…pests." He placed the unlit cigar between his teeth then plucked it out between two fingers and waved it around. "You know, like a...*cómo se dice*...ghostbuster." He chuckled at his joke.

"Right," I said. "So you need someone who will cleanse the house, try and convince the spirit to leave?"

"I don't know what you do or how you do it," he said with a handsome smile. "I just know that my wife and I are at our wit's end. We would like peace and quiet, and we would like it to begin tonight."

Bibi and I exchanged looks. Behind him, away from his stare, she shook her head, a silent message that she didn't want to do it.

But the man was a customer, and he needed a service, a service I had not yet provided to anyone but always knew would one day come. Presuming his house cleansing didn't involve demonic possession. For that, he could contact the Archdiocese of Miami, as only those who believed in the Devil could fight the Devil.

I wasn't sure I did and hadn't for ten years now.

"Is the presence haunting your home a dark one?" I asked just to be sure.

"Dark?"

"You know, a negative energy? Is it causing anguish, arguments between you and your wife? Are bad things happening? Any bad smells?" I tried clarifying.

The man smiled again in his charming way. "I'm sorry, what is your name?" He stepped closer to me.

"Queylin," I said. It sounded no different than Kaylin. Why my mother decided to spell my name this way and curse my school years, I would never know.

"Quey*lín*," he pronounced it with an accent on the last syllable to my annoyance and extended his hand. "My name is Dr. Alberto Rivera. *Mucho gusto.*"

"*Encantada*," I replied.

I caught the scent of aftershave. His shoes were Italian leather. His jawline sported a closely-cropped white beard. He was handsome in an old world way, and I could see him strolling the cracked, colorful tiles of an old home in Havana.

But when his hand slipped into mine, it felt cold. "I need someone, and I need them tonight."

"I understand," I said, pulling my hand away, "but to find you the right person will take time. I need to call around."

"What about yourself?" he asked.

"Me? I..."

Don't have that skill? Present myself as having spiritual gifts through clothes, tattoos, and personal narrative when the truth is I'd never seen a single spirit?

"*Señorita*, I have a lot of money to pay, provided the person is qualified to do the job. I live at the Harding Estate in Palmetto Bay. Surely you can find someone quickly, no?"

The Harding Estate? Most spiritualists would give anything to investigate this famous home that had sat abandoned for several years when I was a teen. I remember trespassing the property just to climb their big banyan tree.

"Oh. I had no idea the house was now occupied. How wonderful for you!" I smiled.

What a lucky son of a bitch.

Dr. Rivera's deep brown eyes were the kind that could see right through you. "Except for the ghosts, *está bien*, I suppose." He shrugged then looked over at Bibi.

He caught her off-guard, as she stood staring at him with her port-wine stain in full view, which was why she'd turned her left cheek a moment later.

"What about you, *niña?*" Dr. Rivera asked.

17

"Me?" Bibi gripped her clear quartz pendant shyly. "I only do consultations in the store."

"Very well, then," Dr. Rivera said, tipping his chin and turning for the door. "I'm sorry to have bothered you. I will find someone else to help me, unless you can recommend someone?"

"Wait…"

This was what I'd always wanted, a chance to prove myself, and at a beautiful historic Miami home, no less. There was no harm in checking it out. I would call Samuel and let him know I'd be home a little late.

"I'll go," I told the man. "As soon as I close up shop, I'll stop by and do a quick assessment before deciding. You said you had a wife?"

He must've found my suggestion amusing, because he suppressed a quiet laugh. "Yes. You needn't worry about me, Quey*lín*. But by all means, bring someone along if it makes you feel better."

He looked at Bibi again, gave her face a moment of extra attention the way most people did when they first saw her birthmark.

"We will see you soon?" the old man asked.

"Yes. But Dr. Rivera?"

He turned to look at me.

"If I can't speak to your ghosts," I said, as doubt crept in. "If the job requires a more qualified individual, I'll refer you to someone else tomorrow. You can pay me for the hour of my time. Does that sound fair?"

"More than fair. Do you need the address?"

"I know where it is. Thank you."

Everyone knew where the Harding Estate was. It had a reputation for being haunted. In fact, it was probably the famous *Dama de Blanco* making her presence known—

the infamous woman in white. The thought of possibly meeting this ghost excited me beyond reason.

Still, I shouldn't have accepted.

I should've referred him to one of my more qualified staff members, or give him the number to any of Miami's paranormal societies. But I couldn't. I was stubborn and needed to do this. For myself.

I was eager to prove my worth. I was also crazy. Either way, I'd be visiting the famous Harding Estate tonight at the owner's request to get rid of unwanted spirits. Baptism by fire.

And that made me a *bruja* of sorts.

A lucky one at that.

THREE

I sat in my car at the Taco Bell on US-1, scarfing down a dollar burrito. I'd read articles suggesting that a vegan diet helped open psychic intuition and had been doing all I could to develop that, but I needed food.

Beef burrito it was.

Also, my bank account had less than a hundred bucks in it. Even though tomorrow was Sam's payday, he'd need most of that for his trip to Chicago tomorrow for the dental conference.

"Hey, babe." He answered my call with that low rumbly laugh I loved. "So, now you're a ghostbuster?"

I'd texted him the minute Dr. Rivera had left, telling him about the strange visit.

I laughed, too. "Tell me if you've heard this one before…an old man walks into a new age shop…"

"Was he a hot old man?"

"He looked like my grandfather."

"Okay, good. So, the Harding Estate, huh? I didn't know anyone lived there. Thought an historic society ran it."

"Shows how much we know."

"Do you need me to come with you?"

"I'll be fine. You need to pack tonight. I bet your suitcase is still empty."

"Uh…of course not. Whatever do you mean? It's full of clothes and toiletries for the next five days. Yeah, that's it."

I laughed. "Babe, you leave at 5 AM. You need to get packing already."

"Throw in a few shirts, five underwear, one pair of shoes. I mean, come on, Quey," he said. "No big deal. Seriously, I'd rather you not go alone."

I sipped from my water bottle. "He has a wife. Besides, I'm not staying long. I told him if I didn't feel I was the right person for the job, I'd refer him to someone else tomorrow."

My husband fell quiet. I knew he was questioning my craziness. "Babe…"

"Yeah."

"Why are you doing this? You could ask Rain or Maggie, any of your staff who've done this sort of thing before."

"I don't know. A personal challenge, I guess."

"Who cares if you can see ghosts or not? I love you either way."

"I know, Sam, but I've always wanted to do this."

"Queylin, it doesn't make you any more special than you already are. You know that, right?"

"I get it, Sam."

"You're already perfect to me."

"Thank you, baby."

Samuel wanted me to drop this personal challenge, my obsession with the "other side." But I'd always been on a quest for evidence. Millions of people could not be lying about their psychic experiences. Sure, a few were charlatans, but most could not be faking it.

There *was* life on the other side.

And I wanted proof.

If I never faced real ghostly activity, I'd never know if I had the gift or not. The house I'd lived in all my life— my parents'—was not haunted in any way, and if it was, I'd never been aware. Our apartment in Coconut Grove was as unremarkable as black ants. Or white sheep.

"It'll be good for me," I added.

"Okay."

"Seriously, it will."

"Okay. But if I'm asleep when you get home, wake me up. If you want to tell me about it, that is."

"I will."

"And if you want anything else, too. Heh, heh."

I smirked. "As if there's any waking you once you're asleep."

"If it means getting some before I leave for five days, I'll wake up. Trust me."

"We'll see. Love you, babe. Wish me luck."

"Good luck. But you won't need it. You make your own luck every single time."

And this was why I loved my husband. He got me, weirdness and all. He was right, though—I'd always had a way of making things work out for me. Rain told me once it was because I was a latent witch. They said I'd been manifesting my dreams all my life like a boss without realizing it. I thought maybe I was just persistent and hardworking, but maybe it was both.

I spent my last few minutes before the appointment searching videos on YouTube about the Harding Estate. I found videos of paranormal investigators checking the place out when it used to be owned by the historical society for twenty years.

In one, several orbs were seen floating through rooms. In another, someone pointed out a dark shape hovering in the corner. One woman investigator said she felt a female presence tap her on the shoulder, but there were no full-body apparitions or appearances from *La Dama de Blanco*.

I wanted to sit and watch them all before going to the house. But I had to get cranking, so I wolfed down the rest of the burrito, turned the engine of my Kia Soul, and headed down Old Cutler under the cover of banyan tree darkness.

Miami didn't have many remote areas left, but Palmetto Bay boasted a few good ones. The road to the Harding Estate was twisty and winding, and I had to check my map app a few times to make sure I was going the right way. Finally, I arrived at tall double iron gates.

One was open.

Slowly, I drove through, tires crunching onto gravel. I was off the beaten path now and opened up the car windows to take in the beautiful tunnel of trees leading to the main house.

After a while of driving underneath a unified canopy of countless trees, it emerged from the murkiness—the Harding Estate—named after the land developer who'd built it in 1919. In those days, there'd been nothing out here but this mansion and a mangrove jungle. Even now, a hundred years later, there was little out here but trees.

What was it about this land that had kept so pristine? When gorgeous, out-of-control Miami mansions had been constructed for miles around, this one still sat solitary facing the bay like some lonely ghost.

I pulled all the way up to the house, rolling around the circular driveway before cutting the engine and stepping out. The air smelled like ocean, and royal palms on either side of the house swayed in the salty breeze. The French colony gas lanterns on either side of the front entrance were lit, which made me smile. I'd trespassed here with friends back when the house was unoccupied and always marveled at how beautiful they were. Dark and abandoned, but beautiful.

At the front door, I took a deep breath.

Here we go.

I allowed myself to imagine that I was a well-known psychic healer called to this home after the owners had heard of my talents, rather than the truth—they'd randomly walked into my shop, desperate for the first idiot they could find.

A shadow passed over me. I looked up the rock exterior to find a feminine shape skirting past a second-story window. It closed the wood shutters and turned off the room light.

The Lady in White.

Doubt it. The wife, most likely.

I rang the doorbell.

In the quietude of the front porch, I listened to the trees rustling in the wind and wondered if any of Dr. Rivera's restless spirits watched me now. My skin prickled with goose bumps at the thought of what I was about to do, and for a moment, I considered leaving a note saying I couldn't go through with it.

You're not a medium, Queylin.

Stop pretending.

But everything I'd ever read said that *everyone* could be born with psychic abilities. You only had to cultivate them. I could do this. I just had to believe in myself.

On the other side of the iron door, footsteps shuffled closer. I heard a latch slide. The large door opened, and there stood Dr. Rivera, cigar clenched between his teeth, only this time, it was lit.

"There she is! Won't you come in?" He stepped aside, holding the door open.

I stepped into the house, and my jaw dropped. "Oh, my."

"You like it?"

"It's beautiful."

Sweet baby Jesus in Heaven, the place was a 1950's Havana dream resurrected from the past. The floor was made of checkered green and cream Mediterranean tiles instead of Dade pine like so many old South Florida homes. Potted *areca* plants were in every corner, colorful paintings of Cuban landscapes and *rumba* dancers graced the lemon walls, and soft sounds of a *son cubano* played in the background as if coming from an old record player.

"I never imagined it would look like this on the inside."

"My wife, she's an artist. Used to sell her paintings at art fairs years ago. You could say she made this place her own." Dr. Rivera closed the door and led me deeper into the house.

"Kudos to her," I said. "All the online photos show the house falling apart."

"Well, I'm a retired therapist, you see. I saved quite a lot to purchase this place one day."

"And you did an amazing job."

"I'm so glad you like it. *¿Quieres refresco o café?*" He offered soda or coffee like any good Cuban host or hostess.

"No, thank you. I just ate. Where's Mrs. Rivera?" I asked.

"She'll be down in a minute. We don't have many guests. I think she's nervous about meeting you."

"Me?"

"Well, she's nervous about discussing the issue. Barbara doesn't like to talk about the…happenings, shall we say?" His smiling eyes disappeared into little crinkles.

"You mean spirits?" I cocked my head. "Why not call them what they are?"

He nodded, cigar bobbing between his teeth. "You will find we are very old school, as you kids say. Millennials, they talk about anything. But us, you know…we are Catholic."

Ah, understood. Talking about spiritual matters was considered taboo in some families if it didn't jive with *la Biblia*.

"But Catholics believe in the Holy Spirit."

"You say that like you are not Catholic?" He raised a bushy gray eyebrow.

"Me? Well, I…was raised Catholic, but I don't practice anymore."

"What *do* you practice then?"

I bristled.

Wasn't sure why.

After all, it was a fair question for someone hired to deal with the spiritual world, but it felt too personal. I hadn't explained my conversion from good ol' Catholic girl to experimental spiritualist to many people. It was hard enough looking my parents and grandparents in the eye, two generations who'd fought hard for the chance to preserve their established ways in a new country, that I didn't entirely walk their path.

I couldn't tell him that, more than anything, I studied manifestation of personal goals. Prayer without the God quotient. I spoke to the Universe and made it do my bidding.

Fine, I practiced witchcraft.

But the good kind. Herbs and candles and oils and setting intentions through meditation. But people like Dr. Rivera heard "witchcraft" and wrongly assumed I was in a Satanic cult. Problem was, you had to believe in Satan to be in a Satanic cult.

"I'm finding my way right now," I said.

He studied me a long time. What the doctor was thinking was a mystery, but it probably fell along the lines of Latino family judgment—a thing in my life.

"I never said we were *practicing* Catholics," he said in a low voice, staring at me. We all go our own ways, *sí?*"

I nodded. Whatever that meant.

When I didn't reply, he pulled his gaze away, leading me down a narrow hallway. I felt out of place. I tried getting the conversation back on track by clearing my throat.

"Believe it or not, the spirit world is a normal part of everyday life, Dr. Rivera." I said it more to calm my nerves than to convince him of anything.

"The spirit world," he replied, pointing a finger in the air, "is nothing but an overactive brain, *señorita.*"

FOUR

I wouldn't argue with the patriarchy today.

Thirty years surrounded by Cuban men of all ages—my father, uncles, brothers, and grandfathers—taught you that sometimes, it was best to stay quiet. No matter what you tried to make them see, they were always right. In their minds. Especially Dr. Rivera, a psychiatrist, who'd made it his life mission to study the brain.

The music grew louder, as we came into a Great Room with tall ceilings filled with more paintings and brightly colored ceramic frogs, lizards, and a gorgeous mosaic coffee table. There on a large, classic *mueble* of dark wood like my grandparents used to have was an old 1940s-looking radio.

"You have one of those?" I ran my fingertips along the old credenza. "Is it your family's?"

"It came with the house, along with that short wave radio." He pointed to another old wooden box. "We brought nothing from Cuba but the clothes on our backs. You should know this."

Heyyy.

"Of course, I do," I said. Every Cuban descendant knew the exiles—many of them doctors, lawyers, teachers, professionals of all kinds—had come to the

States with nothing after leaving it all behind. They'd had to re-earn their degrees and start all over from scratch, re-proving their worth a second time.

It was any wonder they were still sane and thriving sixty years after Castro's revolution tore their world apart. Me, I'd only done four years of college and felt drained.

"So, how do you plan to address our problem, *señorita?*" He sat on one end of a long tufted sofa and gestured for me to sit on the other.

Not wanting to encourage a longer visit than necessary, I perched myself on the edge only. "Well, first I'm going to take a look around. What can you tell me about the haunting?"

"The haunting," he repeated.

"Yes, the manifestations. Your *ghosts*," I said just to bother him.

"*Bueno, vamos a ver.* My wife wakes up screaming in the night. She suffers psychological disorders brought on by childhood separation."

"Oh, I'm sorry."

"She's had it since she arrived in Miami as an eight-year-old in 1961. Part of the Pedro Pan Operation. You should know that, too."

"I know what Pedro Pan is," I said, trying not to sound indignant. He was judging me again. The old ones always had to make sure the new generation knew their Cuban-American history. So it would never repeat itself.

"Good, I was just testing you, *niña*." He smiled. "Your generation calls it PTSD. Post-traumatic stress dis—"

"I know what PTSD is, too," I interrupted with a short laugh. "Sorry. So where does the spirit activity come in?"

"Her screams prompt other screams."

"I beg your pardon?"

He planted both feet on the floor and leaned toward me. "When she wakes up screaming, it triggers something else to scream in the house. Sometimes, there's crying. Sometimes, things move."

"Move?"

"Yes. Objects fall to the floor. Of course, this could very well be the ideomotor effect, or mass hysteria."

My eyes felt like they would pop. "Oh, wow. Does this happen often?"

"More often than I would like."

"Which part of the house should I concentrate on most?"

"I would prefer not to answer any more questions. I would rather you give me your own impression of the house, if you don't mind." He puffed on his cigar again.

He was testing. Withholding information so that I, the talented psychic—after all, I ran a new-age-medium-mystical-arts shop—could tell him where the activity was located.

He didn't trust me.

But I wouldn't let him intimidate me. I would focus my energies, explore the house, and get a sense of where the trouble areas were. Based on gut instinct, I supposed. It was all I had.

"Do you mind if I get started then?" I asked. "I only have an hour."

"You have a husband?"

I looked at him.

If he didn't want to provide me with any info, why should I give him any? *Yes,* I wanted to tell him. I had a big strong man, one that would arrive at a moment's notice if he tried anything funny. One that would kick his old man ass in a heartbeat if the need should arise.

"Yes, I do."

"Why isn't he here with you?" he asked, insinuating that a proper husband should always accompany his frail wife to the home of weird old men.

"He had to pack." The moment I said it, I regretted it. Dr. Rivera didn't need to know anything personal about me or Samuel, especially that he was leaving town.

"Ah, a traveling businessman."

"You could say that."

Telling him that my husband was a dental hygienist would be a mistake. He'd only shame us and say the occupation was a woman's job. That Samuel should be a dentist or a maxillofacial surgeon instead. I knew his kind.

I stood and moved through the house, aware that his eyes were following me, glad I hadn't worn anything that might've been misconstrued as sexy or overly feminine. Not that it should matter, but men like him would take that as permission to stare even more.

The home had no open kitchen. Old homes like these had hidden kitchens with service pantries, areas where staff would cook and prepare without being seen from the dining room.

I entered the dining room and took note of the slow-twirling ceiling fans with blades in the shapes of palm fronds, as well as the bright blue curtains. The table was formally set for three, including dinner fork, salad fork, shrimp fork, every other fork you could think of, plus wine glass, water glass, and maybe even a glass for me to cry my tears into, they were so damn rich.

It made me feel I would never live in a house like this, not in a million years. Not even with all the opportunities I'd been handed.

Dr. Rivera's voice startled me. "We were hoping you would join us for dinner."

"Oh." How had he moved into the room without making a single noise that way? I pressed a palm to my heart. "Thank you, but I can't. *Muy amable.*"

He shrugged, opened a cabinet in the hallway to move a liquor decanter a millimeter to the left, then closed it again.

Once my heartbeat settled, I resumed my walk around the house. Where was his wife? It occurred to me that perhaps he'd lied and here I was alone with a strange man in a house far removed from civilization. Considering Dr. Rivera had asked where my husband was, the thought made me pause.

Quickly scanning to see if he was following me, I found him lingering just outside the room, so I opened a random door and stepped inside.

Once my eyes adjusted to the darkness, I found myself standing in a ballroom that hadn't been decorated like the rest of the house. Stacks of chairs were covered in fabric, round tables leaned on their sides against the walls, and an eerie mustiness filled the room.

The Harding Estate's ballroom.

For a moment, I imagined this space full of people in the 1920s enjoying a cocktail party, waltzing on these parquet floors. I saw them perfectly in my mind's eye, and then I saw the emptiness.

A certain stillness that belied the relative activity going on in the rest of the house.

Were there ghosts here?

I unfocused my vision and tried to see through the atmosphere. Maybe this would be the one time I finally saw them. But nothing materialized except a sense of self-pity, and before I could start feeling sorry for myself, I slipped out a service door and ended up outside.

I was on the veranda, the back porch where multiple rocking chairs were lined up in a row, and the outer walls looked like they were made of coquina, a hard-but-porous, crushed-shell material harvested from the shores of Florida beaches.

I'd only explored one corner of the home and already I felt disoriented, flushed, and overwhelmed. The Harding Estate was expansive and confusing, and I would definitely need more than one night to peruse its corridors.

The cellar, a rogue thought hit me.

Yes, this house had a cellar. I'd read about it in articles and heard the ghost investigators mention its existence in their videos I'd watched earlier. In the old days of Prohibition, it'd been used to store illegal spirits.

A French patio door opened, and Dr. Rivera stepped through onto the veranda. So much for exploring the home by myself. "Finding anything so far?"

"I'm just getting a feel. Does this house have a cellar? I thought it did," I asked.

"A cellar..." He looked out into the night. Just beyond the reaches of the patio lights was Biscayne Bay, its soft waves whispering across the wide lawn. "It used to, but it was flooded during Hurricane Andrew."

"So, there's no cellar now," I clarified.

He turned to me, as if he'd forgotten I was here. "Correct. Not since 1992. The historic society had it filled and sealed." He stared at my face, his eyes roving over my features, then he inspected me from head to toe.

Ick.

"Nice. Well, am I, uh...going to meet your wife?" I asked. Because if he didn't produce a woman soon, I'd probably be going without concluding my investigation.

Dr. Rivera seemed a nice enough man, just old-school in a way that made me uncomfortable.

"Yes, she's eager to meet you," he said, snapping out of it and stepping into the house again. "Go ahead and explore. See the garden. There's a statue there you might find interesting. I'll go find my wife, okay?" He blew out a puff of the sweet-smelling smoke and closed the patio door.

I blew out a long breath. Why was I here? Ah, yes, because Queylin Sanchez-Gold could often be a hard-headed woman.

This would be a good time to do a simple cleansing, ask my spirit guides and angels for protection, and burn some sage. I set down my purse and began to pull out some goodies I'd packed.

Something in the distance caught my attention. At first, it was a light—a burnt, yellowy light glowing through what seemed like aged, dirty glass. Then I saw the shape behind it. A pale human contour standing perfectly still on the lawn.

Ice spread through my veins.

I stared at it, my eyes adjusting to the darkness, gazing on with unfocused vision until I realized it wasn't a spirit standing there checking me out but some sort of solid statue.

Picking my bag up, I walked toward it. As much as the house reeked of impeccability on the inside, on the outside, the lawn was overgrown, and my sandaled feet itched as I walked through the tall, unkempt grass.

The closer I moved to the strange humanoid shape, the clearer it became. The statue was of a beautiful winged angel holding a lantern. It was neither male nor female and smiled with cherubic innocence. I thought of Rain and knew they would love it.

The angel's face looked troubled or serene, depending on where I stood.

My senses took in the surroundings—the lovely night, the crickets, the faraway sounds of tree frogs, the soft swishing of the water's edge a mere hundred feet away. This was quintessential Miami charm—mysterious gardens and angel statues, moonless ocean and strange houses, discussions of religion held in old houses while slow Cuban rhythms lulled you, European cultures clashed with Caribbean ones, blending with tropical beauty and Tequesta lands that never should have been tamed to begin with.

It was all here, and the angel knew it with their secretive smile. Staring at the statue, studying their genderless beauty, I felt sadness.

Longing.

Uncertainty that he would ever come home.

But who? Samuel? Of course he would come home. He always came home. Where was this doubt coming from?

I had studied enough paranormal investigations to recognize what could be happening. I might've been channeling something else, someone else's emotions. In fact, I was certain that if I closed my eyes and focused hard enough, drove away all distractions, that I would open them to find a disembodied spirit standing right in front of me.

"I ask Archangel Michael for protection, Archangel Gabriel to help me communicate," I muttered as a quick charm.

Around me, the air tingled with something I couldn't describe. Some kind of energy. I felt like I stood on the edge of a cliff about to jump to jagged edges below. Someone was nearby. *Or it could be the ideomotor effect, mass hysteria, or carbon dioxide poisoning,* I could hear the doctor man-splaining in my head.

"Who are you?" I asked.

I waited for a reply.

With baited breath, I waited, a thousand percent certain that I would find a person standing there watching me when I opened my eyes. My hands shook, my breath hung suspended inside my throat.

I opened my eyes.

But there was no one.

I sighed. Any pride I'd experienced left my chest like a deflated balloon. I was no one to believe I held special powers. Powers to reach them. Talk to them. See them. I was a regular person, and my husband was right, I didn't need to see them to be special. I was already special to *him.*

Wasn't that enough?

No, it wasn't. I wanted this. But I couldn't make myself turn into someone I wasn't. Time to pack my stuff and call it a night. I was not a spirit medium, no matter how much I wanted to be, and felt like an ass for believing I could help these people.

Just then, however, a chilly breeze coiled around me. Something made me stop. And look up. It was the lantern's dim light growing brighter.

FIVE

It grew then dimmed a bit, then glowed again—pulsating in the gloom of the disheveled garden. This happened three times then stopped.

Part of me told me to get the hell out of there, this wasn't normal. Another told me to stop. *Just stop with your imagination, Queylin.*

Faulty wiring was the cause, more than likely.

It was an old house. The salty air probably didn't help the outdoor electrical circuits either. Mesmerized, I stood still, watching the light, realizing I never burned sage, sprinkled salt, or got around to doing any of my rituals before the statue distracted me.

The night felt balmy. Rain clouds began moving in. Not unusual for a November night in Miami. From somewhere on the other side of the house, the air conditioning unit turned off, amplifying the silence even more. The fluty sounds of the *son cubano* echoed from deep inside the house.

Behind the statue, the canopy of the massive banyan tree of my youth rustled in the wind. Banyans always looked like prisoners to me, serpentine roots reaching for the earth like heavy chains. I couldn't shake the loneliness while staring at it.

"Someone here?" I whispered.

Only sounds of nature shuffling in the night replied.

Walking past the statue, I moved into further darkness toward the tree. My whole life, I'd loved strolling through trees at night, in gardens, parks, and cemeteries. As a teen here with friends, we'd trespassed on these grounds, climbed this exact banyan. There was something timeless and serene about it. The Harding Estate's grounds were exceptionally wild and beautiful.

I stopped at the banyan and stared at it, studying its complicated network of roots. I couldn't explain why I felt isolated, forgotten even, and wondered if something about the tree was bringing out these feelings in me. I had no reason to feel this way.

I'd been married three years now to a wonderful man, one who knew how to make me happy. Still, I couldn't shake the feeling that he'd left me here to fend for myself, but that didn't make sense, since he'd asked if I needed him to come along.

Ripping my gaze away, I walked around the yard, my senses on full alert. Even the sweet smell of humidity felt magnified. Besides the huge banyan, smaller banyans surrounding it, and the angel statue, there wasn't much in the yard except a couple of stone benches and lots of overgrown vegetation, but every so often, I'd run into wild orchids hanging from random braches and bushes.

I headed back to the statue, examining it from behind now. The angel's wings pointed up, its drapery filled with dirt, moss, maybe even mold. There was a crack from one shoulder to where it connected under its armpit. As I came around to gaze into their beautiful face once again, something stopped me.

A word.

You.

Before I could analyze where it'd come from or what it meant, something flew toward me. A rush of air preceded it—whatever it was—and my hair blasted back away from my face. Something invisible and angry slammed into me, knocking the wind right out of my lungs. I hit the ground backwards and cried out, my fingers gripping tall blades of grass in an effort to gather my bearings.

What the hell?

There'd been nothing there!

My breasts felt sore from the impact, and my whole torso ached with a blunt tenderness I'd only felt during my period. Holding onto the statue's pedestal, I scrambled to my feet, chest heaving, lungs gasping for air. I was shaken to my core.

Immediately, I scanned the grounds to see who—or what—might've attacked me. I'd heard of owls and bats living in primitive areas of Miami but being a city girl, I'd never seen one. But did owls or bats go around smacking people in their chests? There was enough ambient light to see what would've caused it, yet I'd seen nothing.

Nothing at all.

I stood up and caught my breath, grasping for any explanation. Had I imagined it? No, of course not. I'd been shoved by someone. Yes, *someone*. As exciting as the prospect of coming here to investigate the Harding Estate might've sounded a few hours ago, now I reconsidered.

I'd felt hands—actual hands—pushing me.

Shit. I should've come with someone more experienced. Things like this happened when I insisted I could handle them, when I actually wasn't prepared for them. I picked up my bag and slung it over my shoulder, getting ready to head back to the house when I stopped cold in my tracks.

"Jesus Christ." I pressed a palm to my chest. The silhouettes of a man and a woman in a wheelchair stood against the flood lights of the house. "I didn't see you there."

The woman, obscured by shadows created by backlighting and a wide-brimmed sun hat, wore a long skirt and a ruffled top, but I couldn't see her face very well. I didn't need to see her face to realize she was very sick. I moved toward the couple until the light shone on the doctor's very ordinary, non-ghostly features.

I breathed out a sigh of relief.

"Sorry to startle you," Dr. Rivera said. "I wanted to introduce you to my wife. Barbara, this is Quey*lin*? Sanchez?" He cocked his head at me.

"Yes. Queylin Sanchez-Gold. Hello," I said, wiping my hands on my jeans to get rid of the dirt from the fall. I extended my hand toward the woman. "Nice to meet you."

The woman made no attempt to shake my hand, and I felt silly trying to engage someone so severely disconnected. I suddenly felt very sorry for Dr. Rivera that he had a wife with special needs.

"She cannot speak," he explained, touching her shoulder, gently fixing the angle of her hat.

"Oh. I'm sorry," I replied, unsure if that was the proper etiquette when meeting someone incapacitated as Mrs. Rivera was.

When he adjusted the brim of the hat, the lower half of her face appeared in the light, and I saw a fair amount of makeup to enhance pretty lips and apple cheekbones. But she was clearly disabled, though I was happy to see that she at least smiled. Her arms and legs, hidden by long sleeves and skirts and frozen in her chair, seemed thin. In younger years, she must've been beautiful. Even now, she was pretty in her own way.

Dr. Rivera smiled sadly.

"This is why we moved here," the doctor said. "For fresh air, a little distance. It's also why she paints. And sculpts, and creates." Dr. Rivera looked at his wife so lovingly, I saw him in a new light. "She's an extremely talented artist."

"I've noticed." I smiled. "The art all over the house is absolutely stunning." I wondered if Mrs. Rivera could hear anything I said, if she could appreciate my compliment, or if she was completely disconnected to the world outside her mind.

"Are you alright? I thought I heard a noise as we were coming out," Dr. Rivera asked.

"As a matter of fact, no. Well, yes, I'm fine," I stuttered. "But something hit me."

"Hit you?" His eyebrows showed genuine concern.

"Yes, I was standing here admiring your garden statue when out of the blue, something pushed me backwards and I fell." Saying it out loud felt validating, but now I was keenly aware of how crazy it sounded.

"Oh? Any idea what it might have been?"

"I don't know, doctor, but considering why you called me here, I have a few theories."

He pressed his lips together in the first sign of sympathy I'd gotten from him all night. "This doesn't surprise me. May I ask where you were before it happened?"

"Right here." I walked over to the spot next to the angel statue. "I was standing right here looking at the angel. Its light glowed in a strange way, like pulsating brighter then dimmer. Does that happen often?"

Dr. Rivera looked at his wife, who simply looked forward. "It's happened a few times," he said. "Would you like to come in for a glass of water? Some wine to help calm you down?"

"Oh, no," I said, checking the time on my phone. "Thank you, but I really do need to get going. My husband's waiting for me, and besides, I think I'm not the right person for this. I'll see who else can come and help you." I backed away, signaling it was time for me to go.

It was hard to admit I was way in over my head, but maybe it was for the best.

"Oh, but you're doing fine, *señorita*. You seem to have made more contact with her than most people."

"With whom?" I asked, baffled. Made contact?

"*La Dama de Blanco*. The Lady in White."

"The Lady in White," I repeated, staring at him. "You think that was The Lady in White?"

He nodded. "We're pretty certain it's she who haunts this home, along with a few other spirits we don't know who they are. In fact, this angel…"

"The Lady in White," I said again. "She's the one who hit me?"

He stepped through the grass over to the statue and laid his hand on the angel's hip. "*Probablemente*," he said. "After all, this is her grave marker, ordered installed by her widower from prison after her death in 1921."

My eyes widened. I must have looked insane to him.

"You didn't know?" he asked.

"No, I didn't. I haven't been here in fifteen years," I replied.

I supposed anyone could know that piece of history by digging online. After all, much was written about this famous home built by a New York City millionaire and bootlegger in the early 20th century, but I hadn't exactly had time to research anything before coming over.

I'd watched YouTube videos and eaten a burrito, though.

I narrowed my eyes at him. "Dr. Rivera, I thought you didn't believe in ghosts. The brain overreacting and such."

"Quey*lín*, I believe most experiences can be explained through science. But every so often, something comes along that baffles researchers to no degree, and The Lady in White, for me, is one of those phenomena."

"Have you ever invited other mediums here to try and speak to her?" I asked.

"Yes, several."

"And?"

"Had they been successful, I wouldn't have wandered into your shop, would I?" He smiled that handsome older gentleman smile, but I noticed his teeth were stained with nicotine.

"Fair enough."

"You're the first person besides us she's actually interacted with while I've lived here, and I've lived here fifteen years now. I need you to stay the night, Quey*lín*. So you can experience our experiences for yourself."

"Sir, I'm feeling a little scattered right now after what happened. But I'll come back better prepared. I promise."

"Bring your friend with you."

"Which friend?"

"The one from the store. With the *manchita* on her face. She looked insightful to me."

I wondered how Dr. Rivera could get the sense that Bibi had been insightful from four seconds of interacting with her, but he was right. Bibi was eerily connected with the spirit world. The problem would be getting her to come.

"I'll see what I can do," I said. "I have to go now." *Or lose my mind.*

"Wait a minute. I'll go inside and write you a check for your time."

"It's okay. Next time I see you."

I could have used that check right now, but I needed to put some distance between this house and my brain.

"*Pierde cuidado.*" He said "no worries" in that special way my grandmother used to when she wanted me to feel guilty for turning her down. "Thank you for coming."

Ugh.

Turning, I exited the property through the archway of a stone wall stretching from the house through the garden and into the darkness. I didn't stop until I'd reached my car. Getting in quickly, I cranked the engine and paused to look at the silhouettes of the doctor and his debilitated wife again.

She seemed to watch me through the darkness with eyes hidden beneath her hat, but how aware could she be, really? I drove off the circular driveway, through the tunnel of trees, and passed the front gate.

Only once I'd reached the end of the road, when the streetlights of US-1 finally came into view, reminding me that I wasn't in the middle of nowhere but in a bustling cityscape, did I let go of the massive breath I'd been holding.

SIX

I lay in bed like I always did, husband asleep to my left, soft meditation music playing on my nightstand—when the ghost walked out of the closet.

She wore jeans and a dark-colored top. Her hair was long and blond, and she almost looked like a younger version of myself.

My body froze.

At first, she stalked through the darkness of my room unaware that I could see her, but the moment she felt me tense up (she sensed my fear like a dog), she turned her face and stared right at me.

To my horror, half her face was missing. Or rather, half the skin of her face, her skull exposed with pieces of flesh still attached. But it wasn't until she shifted her whole body and started walking toward me that I screamed.

Hiding my face under the covers, I felt her weight pressing down on me. I struggled to be free, screaming and pushing with everything I had, but she had me pinned to the bed. When she spoke, her voice sounded watery and distant, and toward the tail end of whatever she was saying (I couldn't tell), she sounded like Samuel.

"Babe. Babe, wake up."

My husband hovered over me in the darkness, and it was him I was fighting, as my screams turned to whimpers. I held onto his arms and breathed in the normal, familiar scent of his skin.

"Oh, my God…"

"You okay? What were you dreaming?"

"There was…a woman. Coming at me."

"A woman?"

"A ghost. Her face…it was…forget it."

There was no point explaining the nightmare, because there wasn't anything particularly terrifying about it. Yes, the woman was missing half her face, but my terror was more about seeing a ghost in my room than anything else. Besides, he'd only lecture me that I was taking things too far.

The sleep paralysis didn't help either.

I felt stupid for waking him up.

"I've never heard you scream in your sleep before, Quey. Go back to sleep. Everything's alright. Everything's okay, baby." Strong hands rubbed my arms and pressed against my forehead.

The loving tone in Samuel's voice slowly brought my heart rate down. He curled up next to me, and though I gave the ghost woman another thought or two, my baby's arms and warm breathing finally lulled me back to sleep.

In the morning, my phone alarm went off. I felt the bed space next to me. Samuel was gone. On the bed was a folded sheet of paper. I opened it—

Babe, here's a little guy to fight the monsters. Sorry about your bad dream. I'll call you when I land.

<3

At the bottom, he'd drawn one of his funny cats doing yoga, holding a crystal between his paws. I smiled and pressed the note to my heart.

Holy shit, the dream last night.

I remembered it now. I didn't normally have nightmares, and if I did, I usually recognized when I was having one and woke myself up. But this time, I'd screamed my head off, something that had never happened before. I must've scared the crap out of Samuel.

The Harding Estate was affecting me. I knew it was. When I'd gotten home last night, I'd found Samuel asleep, all packed for his trip, so I hadn't gotten the chance to tell him. Talking to my husband about my day always helped me release negative energy, but this time I'd gone to bed with it all to myself.

I hadn't told anybody about what happened in the garden. As my brain slowly woke to the realization, though, the details of it came crashing to my mind.

I'd been knocked over by a ghost.

Something invisible had come right through that statue and smacked into my body. I knew it'd been real, because my body ached. Arms, stomach, whole torso, especially my chest hurt from the impact.

I got out of bed, showered, and meditated to set good intentions for the day. Then, I dressed for work, dotted Samuel's note with a drop of rose essential oil for love and happiness and put it in my jeans' pocket for the rest of the day.

Goddess Moon buzzed with busyness. What was it about Friday mornings that made *all* the yoga moms show up for class? Because most would be cheating on their diets and having wine this weekend? Then I realized it was a teacher's planning day, and a few had brought their little ones.

I helped a customer pick out her first pendulum (she couldn't choose between an amethyst and a pretty copper one), while her little girl, clinging to mom's legging-clad thighs, couldn't stop staring at me. All my life I'd had an affinity for attracting babies' and little ones' attention, but this child kept gawking at me like I had a rooster on my head.

"Hi." I smiled.

She drew behind her mom's legs.

"Say hi, Mellie," the woman cooed in a high-pitched voice. "She's just tired."

"It's okay," I said.

"I'll take the copper one. You said it's good for divination?"

"Either one. The quartz will give you clearer answers, the copper will have strong magnetic energy."

"Copper then."

"Great." I helped the woman at the register and noticed Maggie, Rain, and Lorena all conferring in the corner, trying not to look right at me, though it was super obvious they were talking about me.

Once the woman left, the store was empty, and I snaked up to my staff. "What's going on?" I asked.

Rain cocked their head. "We know you went to the Harding Estate last night. How was it?"

I looked at Bibi, working on a sketch at the checkout counter.

I hadn't told my staff anything, but Bibi knew, because she'd been here when Dr. Rivera came in. It wasn't that I didn't want them to know, but I felt curiously possessive about the case and didn't want to get bombarded by their advice.

"I didn't say anything," Bibi assured me.

"Sure."

"It wasn't her." Maggie held up her phone to show me what was on the screen—a text from my husband. "Sam asked us to take care of you while he's in Chicago."

"Ugh." I shook my head. No wonder he'd been texting me all day asking when I'd be going back to the Harding Estate and who I'd be taking with me.

No one.

Rain crossed their arms and looked at me with those big blue *gringo* eyes I envied. "Don't be mad, Quey," they said. "He's just worried about you. Said you didn't sleep well last night. What happened? Was it the house?"

I sighed and took a seat on the stool behind the counter. I told them all about the Harding Estate, how Dr. Rivera had strolled into the shop needing assistance and how I'd taken it upon myself to help him.

"I'm shocked that you went." Lorena said, her Day of the Dead skeleton earrings jiggling from shaking her head. "But proud of you."

Lorena knew I wasn't particularly witchy on the inside but always wanted to be. She'd been the one to teach me about meditation when I used to get tarot readings from her a different store. Still, she seemed a little envious, if my Spidey senses were working properly.

I side-eyed her. "Hey, you're the one who told me we all had it inside of us."

"It's true—we do," she said with a little flair of her hand. "But you shouldn't have gone alone. Just like with the living, the dead can carry bad energy. You need to be protected next time."

"I cleared my space, burned sage, all that," I said. Actually, I never got around to doing so.

"Yeah, but…" Maggie swapped dark looks with Lorena. "Girl, just tell us next time, so we can send you off to battle the right way." Her overarched eyebrow hinted that I should think deeper.

"What does that mean?" I asked.

The door chimed. A customer walked in. Maggie and Lorena left to their respective spots without answering my question.

"You know what it means," Rain whispered then turned to the customer. "Hi, welcome to *Goddess Moon!*"

Bibi gave me a knowing look.

Okay, maybe I did know.

Lorena and Maggie, besides excelling at hypnotherapy and reiki, were also practitioners of an underground Miami secret—*Santería*. They didn't go around advertising it, especially since followers of the Afro-Cuban religion worshipped in secret—also because judgmental people loved to give followers shit over it—but they were Santeras.

Meaning, they danced, chanted, kept religious sheds in the backyard containing statues and offerings, spoke a secret African language, worked spells, and yeah, I hated to say this…sacrificed chickens when necessary.

And *they* knew that *I* knew that *they* knew.

I didn't agree with all aspects of the religion, but there was something to be said for their skills at manifestation. If someone wanted more spice in their marriage, they had a love spell for that. If someone needed to keep an ex away, they had a binding spell for that. If a home filled with negative energy needed a *despojo*, they had a cleansing spell for that.

Somehow, Maggie and Lorena made things happen. Call it witchcraft, the power of prayer, or coincidence if your religion was Science—but they did.

Maybe that was why I hadn't called on them for Dr. Rivera's house. Because I wanted to feel, for once, like a case was *mine* to handle. For once, someone had walked into our shop and not asked for the *wink-wink* voodoo queens.

But when I thought about the invisible spirit that had attacked me, I realized it could've been much worse. I had to take someone with me for the next investigation. Not only for my protection but for Sam's peace of mind as well.

I sidled up to Bibi who was rearranging the essential oils in alphabetical order again. "Will you come with me tonight?"

"Where?"

"The Harding Estate."

"Uh, no, Queylin, please don't make me. I didn't like that guy."

"Me neither, but listen, I met his wife. They're just a basic old couple. I don't want to go alone. Please? Besides, he asked for you." I wasn't telling the whole truth about them being a basic couple. There was nothing basic about a woman in a wheelchair whose whole face I couldn't see.

"Even creepier."

"All we have to do is clear the energy, talk to the spirits if we can, ask them to leave, that's it." I moved the rose and yling-ylang oils together.

"That's it? What happens when the ghosts don't want to leave?"

"Why wouldn't they?"

"Queylin, some spirits don't want to go. They become part of the house. Like a light fixture. Or a bookcase." She moved the oil bottles back.

"Look, it's not just for Dr. Rivera," I said, arranging the eucalyptus and tea tree oils together, because hello, healing properties. "I want to do this for me, too."

She smirked at me. "I knew it."

"What?"

"You're on a personal mission."

"How do you know these things?"

"Samuel said you were."

"Damn it." So much for psychic awareness. My husband would give out my social security number to strangers if I let him. "Please, just one night? We get paid for it, we do our best, and we're done."

"We have to sleep there?" She scoffed.

"Yes. That's when the magic happens. Literally. That's when their ghosts go bump in the night, he said."

She thought about it, but Bibi was not having it. "I don't like doing house calls."

"I don't either, yet I babysat you every week when your parents used to go out. So you have to do this for me."

"You did that for my parents, not me. Fine," she snapped. "Only because there's money involved, and I need money. But if we go, we take Maggie and Lorena's kits with us."

"Kits? No, no. We don't have time for kits." Maggie and Lorena often put together ingredients for their "special" clients—mojo bags with herbs like *Rompe Saraguey* for banishing evil spirits, or a traveling Elegua statuette. Spells in a do-it-yourself kit.

"Too late. They already made them for you. Pick me up at seven."

SEVEN

I couldn't wait for Bibi to see the house. She wasn't old enough to have ever trespassed on the grounds like I did during the home's vacancy, but I was sure she'd appreciate Mrs. Rivera's artwork, being an artist herself.

We arrived in time for dinner. This time, a housekeeper wearing a black dress and white apron let us in. I didn't remember seeing her last time. The woman was all of maybe five feet tall, scents of Haitian cooking wafting off her aura, deep set dark eyes that told of secrets.

"Hi. We're here to see Dr. Rivera? I'm Queylin. This is Bibi."

The woman opened the door wide, letting us in, but she didn't speak. Her gaze fell downward in respect or shyness, I wasn't sure. As during my last visit, the home felt alive with a quiet energy that might've emitted from Mrs. Rivera's oil paintings and colorful mosaics. The old-time Cuban music played in the background again.

"Pretty house, huh?" I asked Bibi.

She nodded, wide hazel eyes taking in her surroundings, but she didn't seem convinced.

The wordless housekeeper showed us through the warmly lit home into the formal dining room, the one I had peeked into during my first visit. Dr. Rivera was seated at the table, reading from an actual newspaper, and rose from his seat when he saw us.

"*Buenas, niñas, buenas*," he said, teeth clenched around another cigar. He wore a white *guayabera* this time and slacks just short enough to show off brown dress socks. "Ah, you brought your friend. How nice."

"This is Bibi," I said. "From the store."

"Yes, I remember," Dr. Rivera said, extending his hand. Behind him, his wife sat in her wheelchair, facing a window, staring out into nothingness.

Bibi gave the doctor her hand but didn't shake long before pulling her fingers away. She seemed to hold her breath uncomfortably, as Dr. Rivera studied her cheek again in the most unabashed way. For eighty percent of his personality, the doctor seemed nice enough, if a little old-school, but every so often, he did something, like give us lingering stares, to make himself seem creepy.

Bibi turned her face and took in the details of the ornate room. I could almost feel her holding her breath. The Riveras' wealth could easily have come across as off-putting to some. Even Mrs. Rivera, in her black off-the-shoulder dress with purple shawl and another wide-brimmed hat, was dressed more for the opera tonight than a simple dinner at home.

"*Amor*, our guests are here. Won't you say hello?" the doctor glanced her way, but Mrs. Rivera continued to stare out the window.

It saddened me that Dr. Rivera continued to expect normal social interaction from his wife, but maybe that was part of her therapy—to speak to her as though all was normal—to keep her involved.

He raised his eyebrows at us and sighed. "Please excuse my wife. We do what we can."

"No, of course," I said. "No worries at all."

"Please, have a seat. We were just about to eat." Dr. Rivera gestured to his dining table, clearly proud to be hosting.

"Thank you so much." I eyed the housekeeper who'd come to stand by Mrs. Rivera's wheelchair. She stood next to it protectively, one hand on the disabled woman's shoulder. "What are we having?"

Dr. Rivera snapped with two fingers, and the woman broke out of her reverie, giving me and Bibi a cursory look before disappearing through a door into the kitchen.

Bibi and I looked at each other. The patriarchy was in full effect.

Dr. Rivera waved his cigar around. *"Diri ak djon djon,"* he replied, carefully pronouncing his Creole. "It's black mushroom rice with shrimp. Have you had it before?"

"No, I haven't. Sounds delicious," I said.

"You'll love it. Well, you're a Miami girl."

By that, he meant I should be familiar with the cuisines of various Caribbean nations, which I was. Even though I'd never had this particular dish before, now I realized the housekeeper must've hailed from Haiti.

"Sounds great, doesn't it?" I asked Bibi, trying to engage her. But Bibi sat politely with hands folded in her lap. Seemed like she, the housekeeper, and Mrs. Rivera were all competing for most tongue-tied tonight, leaving me and the doctor to face off on small talk.

"We appreciate you retuning to our home and bringing assistance with you," Dr. Rivera said, dropping a cloth napkin onto his lap. "Where, may I ask, will you be concentrating your efforts this time?"

As he reached for his water, I thought about how to answer the question. "Well, I thought we'd do a simple cleansing tonight, and—"

"Yes, about that," he interrupted. "When you say cleansing, what exactly are you referring to?"

"There's many ways to do it, but usually it involves burning any number of substances traditionally known to clear negative energy."

"I see. And this works?"

"Yes. It absolutely does."

"How do you know if you've never seen it?"

"Who says I've never seen it?" I retorted.

I didn't mean to sound snarky, but he knew nothing about me. For all he knew, I was incredibly psychic and could see dark energy lifting right off people's bodies like black mist rising into the skies. I found his assumption off-putting.

Dr. Rivera may not have liked this cheeky young woman challenging his idea on the inside, but on the outside, he seemed visibly amused. "I don't know. I suppose I am testing you." He smiled.

Calm down, Queylin. I had to remember that he was a paying customer only testing out my qualifications. Still, he could've been nicer about it.

I looked at stony-faced Bibi then let out a sigh. "To be fair, I haven't actually seen it, but I've felt it. A space feels different after you've cleared it."

"How do you know it's not a psychological effect? You perform a ritual, your brain wants to believe it has followed through…and there you go."

"I don't," I replied. "But if believing is half the battle, then who's to say it serves no purpose?"

The doctor nodded, listening.

So I went on. "Prayer, belief in any god, any religion…it all works the same way. It's about intention, the power of thought."

He tilted his glass at me. "The power of thought. And there, we will agree. What about you, miss?" He turned his attention to Bibi. "Do you believe that 'cleansing' a space will clear us of our pesky ghost problem?" The doctor chuckled.

Bibi cleared her throat. "I think it's a place to start."

"And if it doesn't work?" he asked.

"Then, we'll go from there," Bibi replied.

"Fair enough." The doctor stood from his position at the head of the table and stepped over to his wife. He placed her napkin on her lap, gently kissed the top of her head, whispering something to her, then returned to his seat.

It was melancholy to watch. It made me wonder if Samuel or I would ever reach that point of having to take care of each other in this way. When you first get married, you never think of things like this, but we'd promised to love and cherish through thick and thin, and Dr. Rivera, annoying as he could be, had followed through on that promise. For that, part of me praised him.

The housekeeper (or servant, or nurse) brought out the dishes and set them in front of us. Steaming coils of delicious scents rose from the dark rice. I wasn't much into seafood but would eat this plate containing shrimp, not only to be polite, but because it smelled amazing.

"*Muchas gracias,* Lovely," Dr. Rivera said, waiting until we all had our plates before digging in. "*Bon appétit!*"

"Thank you...Lovely?" I asked the woman, unsure.

"Yes, popular Haitian nickname." The doctor winked at me before she could reply. Did he always have this habit of answering for others?

She bowed her head and backed into the kitchen, closing the door after her. I couldn't imagine being in her position of inferiority. Then again, I was making assumptions. For all I knew, Lovely might've been happy to have a job taking care of a disabled woman and cooking meals she loved.

I had to remember that the world did not only exist through Queylin-colored glasses.

"Mmm," the doctor murmured, taking a bite of the *diri ak djon djon.* "This dish is one of my favorites, and Lovely has been making it for me for fifteen years. Since..." His comment trailed off, almost as though he realized he wasn't alone.

Since his wife had fallen ill, I took it to mean. With a sigh, the doctor resumed eating.

"So, Bibi, is it?"

"Yes." Bibi looked up and took a bite of her food, mentally preparing to be interviewed, or so it seemed.

"I am guessing that is a family nickname, or am I wrong?" he asked.

She nodded. "My brother named me that when I was born. He was only two at the time and couldn't say 'baby.' My actual name is Carina."

"Ah, well, Carina," Dr. Rivera said, even though Bibi never gave him permission to call her as such. "Tell me about the *mancha* on your face...the stain. Is that a burn or...?"

I felt Bibi cringe next to me. God only knew how many times she'd been asked this question. I wouldn't blame her if she wanted to hit the "pass" button and go to the next question instead.

Her sigh was barely audible. "It's a birthmark," she replied flatly. "Port-wine stain. I was born with it, hence...the word, birthmark."

I almost choked on my *diri ak djon djon.*

Instead, I gave Bibi a coy smile. "I'm sure you get asked that a lot," I said in an attempt to soften Dr. Rivera's forwardness.

"I do, yeah. All the time. I guess it's natural for people to be curious, but it makes me uncomfortable."

I gave her a sympathetic smile.

"Have you ever thought of having it removed?" the doctor asked, as though he hadn't just heard the part where Bibi expressed her discomfort regarding the topic.

Her sigh was heavier this time. "No. It's a part of me, just like my eyes, my hair, or your silver hair and spare tire."

"¿Cómo?" Dr. Rivera cocked his head like a dog who'd just heard a high-pitched whine.

Some phrases did not translate well between languages, and this was one better left un-translated.

"What she means is that she likes her birthmark." I smiled at her. *Spare tire?* I looked at her, holding down a laugh. "I like it, too. It suits her."

"Thanks, Quey," she whispered.

"Well, it's all in what we believe, isn't it?" the doctor said.

I leaned into Bibi. "Just one night and we're out of here," I whispered.

"I hate you."

"I know, I'm sorry."

Dr. Rivera broke a piece of bread and gave half to Lovely, so she could pass it onto his wife. Lovely stepped out of the shadows to take the bread and give it to Mrs. Rivera who had no interest in food at the moment. Lovely shrugged then stood awkwardly next to the wheelchair, holding the bread in her hands.

I couldn't tell who looked saddest, the housekeeper, the wife, or the good doctor.

After dinner, Lovely (or Lovelie, or Loveli) showed Bibi and me upstairs. We lugged our bags up the old wooden staircase, through a landing boasting an old mahogany bench in front of a curious painting of a semi-nude woman, and up another set of stairs. In fact, most of this hallway contained similar paintings, and some were more explicit than others, hence their more hidden locations.

"Thank you," I said, as she opened the door to the guest bedroom for us, pointed to two sets of white, fluffy towels, then closed the door quietly.

"Thanks," Bibi said.

Once alone in the room, we let out huge breaths. I dropped my bag into a chair and sat on the edge of the bed. "Well, this has been an interesting night."

"You owe me huge," Bibi sighed.

"Dude, I swear he wasn't this creepy the first night."

"He was this creepy at the store, Quey. But for some reason you didn't see it."

"Nah, he's just old," I said, walking around the room, admiring the weird and tacky furniture art. "Loves to hear himself talk. I know the kind. You know the kind."

"Doesn't excuse him."

"Yes, I see that now. But I also wanted to see this house really bad. Aren't you glad you can now say you've seen the Harding Estate on the inside?"

"Yes. So wonderful to see this private home on the water so far removed from civilization, owned by a rude man who doesn't allow women to talk."

"Hey, it's not his wife's fault she doesn't speak. She's sick. He said something about PTSD."

"She's got more than PTSD, my friend," Bibi said, falling quiet for a minute. "It's like she's not allowed to speak."

As we walked around the room, examining the strange furniture, I thought Bibi was being a little judgmental. After all, we'd both witnessed the doctor treat his wife with sweet affection. A man oppressing his woman would not have done that. But she'd done me a favor by coming, so I kept quiet about it.

"There, now we've seen the house. Can we go now?" She scoffed.

"And miss the amazing chance to stay in the gaudy bedazzled bedroom from hell?" I glanced around. "I mean, look at this place!"

Whereas the rest of the house told of Hollywood golden days blended with Caribbean flair, the guest bedroom looked like someone had vomited their fashion jewelry drawer onto every square inch of surface area. The lamps had been stamped with old earrings, the edges of the 1980s furniture were hot-glued with necklace charms—silver cats, gold snowflakes, fake crystals—every style discarded bauble and trinket you could think of.

I mean, major points for repurposing old shit, I suppose. But it made for a very...*eclectic* style.

The curtains were made from denim scraps, but I had to admit those were pretty cool. There were even pockets in some of them, which made me remember my own jeans pocket where I'd placed the love note from Samuel this morning.

Taking the folded paper out, I pressed it to my nose, inhaled the scent of rose oil, and set it on my nightstand—a little something to keep me company through the night.

"Should we get started?" Bibi checked her phone then threw it onto the quilted bedspread made from different patterned fabrics. "This whole room could use a massive smudging."

"Yes. Listen, thank you for coming. I know you didn't want to. And I know I was excited to be here, but now that I am, I don't think I would've taken well to sleeping in this room alone."

"But it sparkles. It glitters."

"Nothing can save it. Not even sparkles."

We laughed and went through our bags, preparing to sage the heck out of the room. Releasing the tension felt nice, if forced. Bibi lit the end of a smudge stick and placed it in her abalone shell. Together, we stood facing east toward the bedroom door.

"You do the honors, little witch," she said.

I smiled. Whereas Bibi was highly intuitive, I, at least, knew something about ritual. If I couldn't bring natural talent to the table, I at least knew procedure.

Closing my eyes, I lifted my palms to the ceiling. "Guardians of the East watchtower, keepers of air, we welcome you into this sacred space. Lend us your intuition and lightness of being."

It was something I had learned to say from the countless books I'd read over the years, and if my Catholic parents ever heard me, they'd disown me. But this was why I'd surrounded myself with like-minded individuals—Bibi, Lorena, Rain, and Maggie—my coven, one might say.

Bibi drew a pentacle in the air with the white sage smoke and waited as I turned south before following suit. "Guardians of the South watchtower, keepers of fire, we welcome you into this sacred space. Please lend us your passion, your drive, and your spirit."

We asked the elements of water and earth to join us, ending with Spirit, the most important one of them all, after which I drew a circle of protection around us using an athamé and imagined us in a bubble of light. Once the circle was cast and the quarters summoned, I asked for anyone whose interest it was to protect us to join us. Angels, spirit guides, ancestors. To protect this room, this home, from any entities that wished to harm us, harm this family. Let them know it was time to move on, time to let this family live in peace.

Bibi and I cleared the room, meditated, and said a prayer together. Once it seemed like we could resume the evening in peace, we closed the spell circle, took turns showering in the adjoining art deco bathroom, and got to bed early.

Tomorrow, we would clear the whole house. We would use Lorena and Maggie's magickal kits and ingredients to wash floors and smudge corners. We would use everything in our arsenal to cleanse this home, and if nothing helped the Riveras, well then we'd pass the torch to someone else.

"I don't like this house," Bibi said with the quilt up to her chin. "There's something here."

"Even after we cleared?"

"Yes. They're keeping their distance," she said, her words sending goose bumps up my arms. "They're not leaving. They're not ready."

How she knew that both freaked me out and fascinated me.

"Then, let's get some sleep," I said. "Maybe we'll have better luck tomorrow."

Bibi was quiet.

I sent Samuel a round of goodnight texts. It was earlier in Illinois. I'd spoken to him on the drive to the

Harding Estate, but now that we were here, I didn't want anything of my own interfering with the home's energy, so I refrained from calling him.

I hadn't turned off the light for more than a minute when Bibi sighed in the darkness.

"You okay?" I stared at the ceiling fan that twirled slowly high above us.

"Sure." She rolled away from me. "If you don't count that woman standing in the corner."

EIGHT

"Woman?"

"Yes, by the door."

Slowly, I turned my head.

It wasn't that I was scared of seeing a woman standing in the corner of the room, but—I was scared of seeing a woman standing in the corner of the room. I'd never done this before. I'd never seen a ghost. Now that the opportunity was here, I wasn't so sure I welcomed it anymore.

As my heart rate kicked up, I tried focusing my fuzzy night vision near the door. A woman. If I relaxed and let my third eye take over, I'd see what Bibi saw, too. However, all I saw was an old bedazzled mirror, a chair holding clothes, and a rack with an umbrella hanging from it.

"I don't see her."

"She's leaving."

As much as I tried to see the shape of a woman moving through the room, I couldn't. My life's frustrations. "Is it Julia Harding?" I asked.

"Don't think so. She's wearing jeans. Julia lived in the twenties, didn't she?" Bibi asked.

"I think so."

"Anyway, she's gone now. Go to sleep, Quey. Sorry to scare you." Bibi settled into bed with another sigh. I could tell this was old hat to her, but to me, my hopes were still lit like St. Elmo's Fire.

"It's fine. I'm more jealous you can see them than anything," I muttered, rolling over and closing my eyes. As if I could sleep tonight.

A woman.

A woman in the room.

It took a long time, but eventually I fell asleep with the covers over my head and body turned toward Bibi. It was times like these that I wondered what my fascination with seeing spirits was all about, and I knew what drove it—fear.

Once something stopped being scary or fascinating, I no longer obsessed over it. But this was one obsession that, no pun intended, had haunted me my whole life.

For hours, I dreamed about the Harding Estate and the cleansing we'd be performing in the morning. I dreamed of going through the motions, getting everything just right. I dreamed about Mrs. Rivera's lips being sewn shut, and about Lovely's tongue being cut from her mouth.

Why didn't these women speak?

In another part of the dream, I saw the two speaking to each other, carrying on a conversation. So they had things to say after all. Why couldn't I hear them? And what were they saying?

I was in the middle of dreaming that an unidentified woman in jeans stalked our room in the middle of the night when I felt a presence near me in bed. I opened my eyes—at least I did in the dream—and found I wasn't wrong. There was someone. I could feel it in the air displacement.

A woman.

A woman in the room. Similar scenario to the nightmare I'd had last night when Samuel had to talk me back to Earth, only this time the ghost hovered over me.

Eye sockets hollow.

Cheekbones protruded, as the rest of her skin drew against her face bones. She wasn't evil, but she scared me anyway.

In her thin hands, she held trinkets and baubles collected over the years. She showed them to me with urgency, as though I should look deeper, find meaning in the items. I wanted to scream—I didn't like having anyone surprise me while I slept, especially a gaunt, desperate ghost. I'd always said I wouldn't mind seeing one as long as it didn't hover over me bedside, but here my fears were coming true.

"Bi...bi..."

I might have spoken aloud, or it might've been in my dream.

"Bibi?"

The woman continued to stare at me with missing eyes, stringy dark hair hanging on either side of her face. Those thin fingers holding that tangled mass of jewelry...

"What do you want?" I asked the dream spirit—at least I thought it was a dream—forcing myself to be brave.

She wouldn't reply.

Couldn't reply, I realized.

Her mouth had been sewn shut, too, just like Mrs. Rivera in my dream and the housekeeper who'd been silenced another way.

Paralysis gripped me. As much as I wanted to run from the skinny woman presenting baubles to me in my sleep, I couldn't move. As much as I wanted to believe these ideas about the women in the house, my rational brain knew they weren't true. Mrs. Rivera had post traumatic stress disorder or some other degenerative disease. And Lovely might have been a woman rescued from the harsh realities of Haiti, had witnessed the hell of earthquakes and famine, and had nothing left to say. Dr. Rivera was kind to them, nothing more or less.

Change your viewpoint, Queylin.

I curled into a ball and rocked as hard as I could until I ripped awake in real life and found myself sitting up in bed. No ghost anywhere in sight. Something outside scraped against the window pane. Branches. Branches in the bay breeze.

"What? What is it?" Bibi startled awake by my jerky movement.

"I saw her."

"Who?"

"The woman in the room."

I reached over to the nightstand and switched on the lamp, scared to see her lurking there, but she was gone. Or invisible now that I wasn't dreaming. I'd sleep with the light on for the rest of the night if I had to, but I was not going back to darkness. I wasn't even sure that she'd been real. Like Dr. Rivera believed, it could've been my brain.

But then, Bibi confirmed it.

"She's still here," she said, staring into the corner of the room. "But leaving now."

"Where? What does she want?" I asked, feeling panicky. What gift did Bibi possess that I didn't, and why? If ghosts were real, why couldn't they show themselves to everyone? One, great mystery of life would be solved, just like that.

"She's trying to tell us something."

"Was this her room at one time?" I panted. "Does she want us to leave?"

"I don't think so. It's more like she's warning us."

"About what?"

"I don't know, Quey. I don't have all the answers," Bibi said, throwing her legs over the side of the bed and pushing her face into her hands.

"Sorry." It was 4 AM and here I was, making demands of a friend who didn't want to be here to begin with. I rubbed my eyes and felt sick suddenly, same as I had after yesterday's nightmare. These new experiences were getting to me.

Scrambling to my feet, I ran to the bathroom, leaned over the toilet, and heaved. Nothing came out but the warm saliva that had filled my mouth a moment ago. If Samuel were here, he'd insist I go home and forget this nonsense right this second.

Bibi stood in the doorway. "You okay?"

"Just give me a minute."

I heaved again, but the feeling passed. Lifting my chin, I breathed in and out deeply to catch my breath. Bibi touched my shoulder.

"Quey, I think we should leave in the morning. I don't like the vibes I'm picking up from this place."

"Which is why they need our help."

Bibi was one of those people who, though blessed with this gift, did not like having it, so it made sense that she'd want to go, but I wasn't ready. Though a ghost had knocked me onto my ass and two others had shown me things in my sleep, I wanted to know what they wanted.

I wanted to help this couple.

All thirty years of my life so far, I never saw spirits. Then, since yesterday, when one of them had slammed into me in the garden, something had changed. Maybe the house's energy was waking up my intuition, or maybe Julia Harding herself had unblocked my third eye chakra, because suddenly, things felt different.

I felt closer to hearing them.

To seeing them.

I stood and washed my face in the sink, rubbing the sleep out of my eyes and spiking cold water from the 1920s faucets over my face. Even the mirror frame had old baubles and buttons glued to it. When I looked into the reflection to gauge how shitty I must've looked...

I saw her.

Sunken cheekbones, long brown hair hanging over her face, cracked lips, and eyes—I couldn't see them but I knew they were there, recessed into the hollowed spaces. Luminous blue-violet, her eyes had been bright at one point.

I couldn't move.

She wrapped her hands around my mid-torso as if to feel how solid I was. As though she missed being real and made of flesh. I pushed her away, feeling solid body, and screamed.

But it was only Bibi standing there, perplexed at what was going on with me. "Quey? What is it?"

"She was...I thought...you were..." I couldn't complete one thought to save my life. All I knew was that my pounding heart would crack a rib any moment now. "Damn it."

"She's with you," Bibi said, her voice sounding distant and trance-like. Her hollow voice startled me, dislodging another shriek from my throat.

I ran from the bathroom and sat on the edge of the bed, rocking myself. I couldn't be afraid. I'd come to this house to perform a service. I'd asked for this. How stupid would it be if the medium they'd hired was too terrified to do her job.

Get your shit together, Queylin.

"Okay…" I said, mustering up courage. "Let's do this. Right now. Let's talk to her."

"I agree. Let's do this, so we can go soon. Stand up," Bibi ordered. "Hold my hands."

I stood and slipped my cold fingers into Bibi's warm ones. In the feeble light of the room, I watched her close her eyes. I closed mine, too.

"God and Goddess, we create this circle to strengthen our energy. Lend us your light and your love…" I'd only heard Bibi summon deities once before when she'd read my tarot cards. Her voice soothed me immediately.

"So mote it be," I said.

"So mote it be. And we ask that the spirit in this room tell us her name if it will serve our higher good and help this family."

We waited a few moments.

Then Bibi said, "Thank you, I understand. We wish you no harm. Is there something you want to tell us before you turn and move into the light?"

Another moment of pause. I tried to hear the conversation going on in another dimension, and for a moment, I thought I heard her voice clear as a bell.

Not ready…

"You have unfinished business?" Bibi asked, and again, we waited. "What are they? Are they yours?"

I knew Bibi was asking about the baubles in the ghost's hands. About the trinkets all throughout the room.

71

"I see. Thank you for telling us. You can leave now. There's a light. Walk towards it and go in peace."

"What did she say her name was?" I whispered.

"She said she can't remember."

How awful. How incredibly sad that a spirit couldn't remember who she was or why she was here. Only that she wasn't ready. Oddly enough, I felt her pain, the urgency for us to know why she wasn't ready. She'd been done harm.

And the harm had been done in this house.

The woman's hollow, pecked-out eyes appeared in my vision. I dropped Bibi's hands and stepped back clumsily. "What was that?" I demanded.

"You can't just break the circle, Quey," Bibi chastised. "Give me your hands."

"I'm sorry. I just...I saw her. I heard her say something," I stammered. "About this house."

"About this room? Jewelry that belonged to her? And others?" Bibi asked.

I shook my head. "No. About women who'd lived in this house. The stuff glued to the furniture used to be theirs." Where had this information come from? I had no idea. It was as if it'd been passed straight into my consciousness from those hollow eyes themselves.

"So this 'art' was made from jewelry of the deceased?" Bibi asked.

"I think so."

"Ugh, that's not creepy at all," Bibi said. "Let us close this circle. Go in peace, so mote it be."

So mote it be. Blessed be. I couldn't vocalize. I'd been so utterly shaken tonight. Here we were, surrounded by items of the dead. No wonder I couldn't sleep. The emotions of the deceased were imprinted on these belongings all around us, and the main impression I got was sadness and anger.

"She's gone," Bibi said.

"Are you sure?"

"Yes."

"Who was she?" I asked.

"I'm guessing she lived in the house at one point, but I don't know the history of the place. I can't tell you who."

"We should look into it tomorrow."

"Doesn't matter who she was, honestly." Bibi stepped into the bathroom and reached for a towel. "What matters is that she move on and find peace, but something tells me she can't do that."

"Why?"

"Quey, you need to accept the fact that sometimes, there's nothing that will help. Some houses, especially these old ones, come with their ghosts. It's a package deal. And anyone who agrees to live there needs to accept that."

I felt what she was saying, but at the same time, I couldn't accept it. I wanted to help. I'd come this far on my spiritual journey for a reason. My impressions of the ghosts so far were that Julia carried sadness, and this other female spirit was desperate to communicate. Both needed guidance so they could move on. But who was I here to help—the living or the dead?

NINE

Despite being awake half the night with me, Bibi woke up early. I got the point—get up, do our thing, then leave. She didn't say much, and I could tell she was upset.

"You okay?" I asked.

"Fine." She pulled up the comforter, drew it over the pillows. "But I'm out of here, Quey."

I smirked. I saw this one coming a mile away. "You're not going to stay and help me cleanse the house?"

"I want to, but I can't shake this feeling. It's like the house doesn't want us here or want anyone to be happy, so I'm not sure a spiritual cleanse will help. You can stay if you want to, just don't stay another night."

I was disappointed, but I couldn't be upset with her. First of all, I'd asked her to come as a favor and she'd already followed through when we performed the basic clearing. Also, last night was stressful for us both. Finally, her shift at the store started at noon anyway, so I understood her wanting to get a move on.

"I don't blame you," I said, watching her gather up her bag and stuff from the bathroom. "You want me to drive you back?"

"I'll take Lyft. But listen…" She faced me and took my hands. "You know what to do, Queylin. You've been training for this your whole life."

I laughed. "You make me sound like an Olympic swimmer."

"This is harder than swimming. Do the cleanse then come home. Okay? But don't linger here anymore than is necessary. Remember what I said: sometimes you just can't help. Plus…"

"Plus?"

"I didn't want to tell you this before, but…"

"But?"

She sighed, shook my hands. Her big hazel eyes implored me. "Your inexperience makes you more susceptible. You know how I can't explain what I feel sometimes? You're going to feel a lot of that. Vulnerability. Don't let the house drag you in."

"Okay," I said. "I won't."

I wanted to feel indignant for her leaving me all alone, especially if she felt I was more vulnerable than usual, but I couldn't. She was well within her right to leave. On another hand, she was right—I could do this. If anyone was ready, it was me. I'd studied the metaphysical arts more than anyone on my team, *because* I hadn't been born with natural talent. I was a veritable *Wicca*-pedia of information.

We followed the musical sounds of silverware clinking against plates to find Dr. Rivera in the dining room having breakfast. Behind him, just outside the window on the back veranda, Mrs. Rivera sat in her wheelchair silently contemplating the bay.

The old man stood and gestured to the extra place settings. "Won't you please join us? We didn't want to wake you."

"I will, but Bibi is leaving. She has work to do," I explained. Bibi's nervous eyes glanced around the room to avoid direct contact with the doctor.

"Oh." Dr. Rivera seemed genuinely disappointed. "I'm sorry to hear that. Did something happen last night? We thought we heard a scream. But that is also a common occurrence around here." He chuckled.

Bibi touched the dining table with her fingertips and looked at me to handle the question.

"As a matter of fact, yes," I said. "We both encountered...a ghost in our room last night. The spirit of a young woman. Do you know who she might be?" I asked Dr. Rivera.

The doctor used his nail to pry something from his teeth. He looked at Lovely who'd come in to refill the doctor's cup and fill ours. "I have no idea, as I have never seen them myself. Did she speak to you?"

Bibi adjusted the bag on her shoulder uncomfortably. "She showed us jewelry," she said, "fashion jewelry. You know, the fake stuff. I think she was trying to tell us something about the room we were in, since, well...there's a lot of jewelry in there."

"Yes." Dr. Rivera nodded slowly. "One day, my wife dumped all her drawers on the bed, and she and Lovely began making art with the stuff she no longer used. Clever of them, *verdad*?"

"Uh, yes." Clever was one way of describing the artistic style. Mrs. Rivera must've been hoarding a *lot* of crappy old fashion jewelry to cover that much furniture.

"So, why do you think the spirit would've shown that to us?" I asked Dr. Rivera. "Is there something special about it?"

"Not that I know of. Like I said, it was old stuff. Rather than throwing it away, she repurposed it. What did she look like? The spirit?"

"I only saw her for a moment, but—"

"She was modern," Bibi finally spoke up and stared at the doctor. "Jeans, T-shirt…not from any other era. She was a white woman, brunette, pretty."

"*Bueno*, you just described every woman in Miami," the doctor said with a chuckle.

Bibi did not laugh. She stared at Dr. Rivera, and I thought I sensed some tension between them.

"Her eyes were bright," I added. It was the only thing I truly remembered from my dream. Even through sunken eye sockets, I remember them staring at me. "A peculiar shade of blue."

The doctor stared at me, narrowing his eyes. "Is that so?"

"I think so. It's hard for me to tell sometimes," I said, nearly adding that I was still new to this, though Dr. Rivera knew nothing about it.

After a minute of gazing at me, he finally tore his stare away. "Anyway, stay and eat, Queylin, while I accompany Bibi to the door."

"Thank you, but I can find my way out." Bibi gave me a final nod, before turning and heading toward the hallway. "I ordered a car."

"Nonsense, I'll see you safely and also have something for your time." He pulled a folded bill from his pocket and handed it to her.

Hesitantly, she looked at the money. Knowing Bibi, she was wondering if she should take it, if it contained bad energy or not. "Thank you," she said after a moment, taking the bill and putting it in her bag. "See you later, Quey. Call me."

"I will."

As Dr. Rivera followed her to the door, I sat at the table while Lovely appeared to place bagels and spreads in front of me. "Thank you so much," I said, giving her a smile. For a moment, my brain remembered Lovely with her tongue cut out, bleeding from the mouth, as my dream had shown me, but now, in person, it was clear she was just a shy, quiet woman, and my imagination was on overdrive.

I cleared my throat. "The, um, guest room is really interesting," I told her. "That must've taken you and Mrs. Rivera a long time to bedazzle all the furniture like that."

Lovely just stood in the corner of the room, unsure if she should reply, smiling softly at the bagels. Maybe she didn't know English, but I didn't speak Creole either, so small talk was a problem.

"Did all that jewelry really belong to Mrs. Rivera? Or did you guys raid Goodwill?" I laughed, reaching for a bagel and smearing cream cheese onto it. Silly question, but it was better than silence with a stranger.

As I ate my breakfast, I thought about the mystery surrounding the Harding Estate. I thought about Bibi's impressions and why she felt the need to leave early. I thought about Mrs. Rivera out on the veranda getting fresh air and taking in the lovely view.

What would she say if she could speak? Were her memories of coming to America that traumatic, or was she on the brink of Alzheimer's and her husband just didn't want to admit it? Was Dr. Rivera controlling like he seemed, or was he sweet like he'd demonstrated on multiple occasions?

Who knew where the truth lay, really, and in any case, it was none of my business. I had to remember that I was here to do a cleansing and not get wrapped up in this family's problems.

Speaking of which, it was time to get to work, and Dr. Rivera was taking a long time to get back to the table. In fact, about fifteen minutes of silence had passed in the dining room with Lovely tending to my breakfast needs.

"Excuse me," I told her, as I stood. "I'm going to see if my friend is okay."

Lovely's perpetually happy daze seemed to dissipate, as her dark eyes filled with blankness. I slipped out of the dining room, through the house, to the front door. Opening it and walking to the front circular driveway, I glanced around at the emptiness.

Bibi had left, and Dr. Rivera might have gone to the restroom or to check on something. I sent Bibi a text: *Thanks for coming with me. LMK how the store is doing later.*

After a minute, she replied: *I will.*

Smiling, I turned and started heading back into the house when something stopped me. Pausing to listen, I heard a sound coming from the side of the house. I closed the door and stepped around the bushes and large windows, following the source of the noise.

For a moment, I could've sworn it was Bibi, but she'd just replied to my text. Was someone crying?

I was met with the large iron gate leading into the side of the house, where the garden stretched for acres across the property. As much as I felt drawn to whatever was behind the gate, I didn't want to get smacked in the chest by Julia's ghost again. Then again, interaction with ghosts was why I'd come. If I didn't face them head-on, I may as well call it a day.

Trying the latch, I found it open, same as last time. I slipped in and closed the gate behind me. The crying sounds seemed to get closer, but it was difficult to tell where they originated. At times, they seemed to be coming from the yard. Other times, from inside the house, through an open window. But it also could've been the wind cooing through a screen.

I stepped over broken flagstones and walked into the dense overgrown vegetation taking up most of the yard. The rogue purple, white, and tangerine orchids sprouting from the trees provided a touch of color and elegance to the otherwise creepy garden.

The angel statue seemed to watch me approach, as if happy to have a visitor again. I imagined living in this house and fixing up this area to make it inviting for guests. I could make an incredible meditation garden out here with a stone bench and a trickling water fountain. Maybe then the angel wouldn't look so melancholy.

Was the angel the one crying?

Pausing in front of the statue, I looked up and watched, waiting for the sobs to resume their chorus in minor key. For a long minute, it felt as though the angel would move this time. After a few minutes of studying the angel and absorbing the silence, I heard it again. Heavy weeping. I closed my eyes and allowed my heart to feel every drop of anguish as though it were my own. Only then would I know who it belonged to. Trust my instincts.

Will he ever return?

Will I raise this baby all alone?

My eyes popped open.

Baby?

Suddenly, the same feeling I'd gotten when the spirit had pushed me over yesterday returned—soreness all around, especially around my chest and mid-torso. I'd been expecting my period all this week, but now I couldn't tell if I was having cramps of my own, or this sensation was a psychic impression I'd picked up from someone else.

Julia Harding. Maybe she'd been pregnant when she took her own life. I hadn't read that anywhere. I hadn't researched too deeply, but that would make sense given the way I'd been feeling. I'd even experienced nausea on several occasions, but who was this person she was waiting for?

"Julia?" I whispered. "Are you okay?"

Unsettling silence spread over the grounds. I could hear every cricket, every worm, every blade of grass rising and settling under the sun's movements.

"Mrs. Harding?"

I could almost hear her answer, *not* of my imagination. I heard her in the breeze, in the distant boat horns, in the lapping of waves against the mangroves. No, she was not okay. She was trapped without options. I felt this in a way I couldn't explain. I felt it deep inside my soul.

The angel's downward gaze seemed to focus on me just then, heavy-lidded eyes snapping to my face, and then…the lantern blinked on.

I gasped, stepping back, wrapping my fingers around a narrow fruit tree. I shouldn't have been out here without my tools, without having performed a cleansing yet. I probably should've gotten on with the job, but this house had a way of sucking me in, catching me off guard.

I remembered Bibi's warning: *don't let the house keep you.* Get my work done and get out. I did not want a repeat of yesterday's psychic attack.

The lantern's light pulsated same as yesterday, brighter then lower, then brighter again. My instincts were to flee the yard, get inside in the house, but I stopped myself.

Stop it. This is what you wanted, Queylin.

The crying intensified.

I followed the sound as best as I could, stepping over rocks, wading through tall grass. The weeping led me deeper into the garden and straight for the banyan tree. The tree I'd always loved. Maybe it was the banyan crying. I stared up at the massive thing, imagining it in this same place a long time ago. This tree had witnessed more changes in the last hundred years than any of us had.

It knew things about the families who'd lived here. About the house that had stood for a century. About the Tequesta who'd lived here long before any of us settlers came along. This tree, and the angel, both told me things about Julia Harding that nobody could have known.

She'd been pregnant.

The information slid into my mind. How did I know? I didn't. I felt it to be true.

And the father...

Jesus...

It all overcame me so powerfully—the emotional pain of separation, the uncertainty, the hopelessness—I doubled over and threw up right on the ground. My hands and knees shook from the sickness, and my stomach trembled. I battled overwhelming thoughts I couldn't differentiate from my own.

When I gathered enough energy to look up, I saw the dirty pair of feet. Then the bright red blood dribbling in a thin line down the inside of her leg, seeping between her toes, dripping into the earth.

Her head tilted to one side, neck broken.

It was Julia, swinging peacefully in the ocean breeze.

TEN

My breakfast rose again, but I tamped it down with gulps of fresh air. I couldn't scream. I was too shocked by the sight. As horrible as Julia looked up there hanging from that great branch, I was too petrified to move.

It took a long time before I could rip my eyes away from the vision, and my limbs felt like Jell-O that'd been left outside after a summer picnic. Why had I always wanted to see something this horrible? I couldn't remember what had seemed so exciting about it. Now I just wanted to run from here.

It was time to do what I'd come to do, then go.

The vision dissipated before my eyes. I backed out of the garden, eyes glued to the spot, making sure she wasn't going to climb down from that branch and follow me home. A stupid idea, I knew, but right now, I felt like anything could happen.

At this point, I was 99% convinced that whatever Julia's ghost did to me yesterday when it slammed into me, it worked. She must've dislodged the calcification over my pineal gland, the gland purportedly responsible for psychic vision. Because here I was—seeing things.

Those ghosts I felt so jealous for never seeing?

There they were.

I reached the house and rushed inside to catch my breath. There was no one around from what I could see, though Dr. Rivera could've been watching from any hidden corner, and I felt like he was. Like I was live on a reality TV show, and audiences were getting a kick out of watching me coil away in terror.

Rushing upstairs to grab my things, I felt like a hundred pairs of eyes were following me. In the middle of the staircase, one particular cold spot blocked my way. It could've been a draft, but I felt like it was a person standing there. Out of the corner of my eye, I thought I'd see them, but they'd only turn out to be a banister, or an open door casting shadows on walls, or paintings of 50s-era women in rumba dresses.

All eyes watching me.

"Not scary, not scary..." I whispered.

I couldn't let anything distract me from my task. And yet I felt like everything in the house wanted my attention.

I reached the guest bedroom and found the bed made and my things neatly stacked on top of the dresser. I attributed this to Lovely tidying things up, and while I didn't think she'd tampered with anything, it still felt weird to know someone had touched my things.

I opened my ritual bag, checked to make sure everything was still inside, and changed into white pants and white shirt. Not that I practiced Santería, but if I was going to incorporate a few of the religion's traditions, then I may as well do it the right way. White represented purity, and that was my goal. Purity of heart, purity of light, positive energy.

With my stuff, I hurried downstairs eager to get away from the guest bedroom and the ghost who lingered there when I stopped cold. Lovely stood by the entrance to the service kitchen staring at me.

"Oh, hello, there," I said.

She didn't reply, just looked at my bag and the clothes I was wearing.

"Do you have a bucket? And a mop?" I asked. I knew that sounded strange, but the first ritual I'd be doing involved literally sweeping ghosts out of the house.

I shouldn't have been surprised when she simply nodded and disappeared down a hall. A moment later, she returned with a red bucket and damp mop inside. So she understood English after all.

"Thank you." I watched her slip back into the service hall, curious wide eyes watching me remove all sorts of bottles the ladies had put together for me on top of a coffee table. I felt a little strange having someone watch me, but I also thought that maybe she was familiar with it all.

Eventually, she slipped out of sight.

I sighed and entered a half bathroom to fill the bucket with cold water then returned to the living room and poured all the bottles into the bucket. Herb blends like *Quita Maldición* (curse remover), *Yo Puedo Mas Que Tú* (for empowerment), *Rompe Saraguey* (negative spirit remover), and other stuff from the *botanica lucumí*.

To begin, I pulled out a piece of charcoal and lit it inside of an abalone shell, along with a sage smudge stick. I knew I was blending all sorts of witchcraft from different cultures, but hell, this house needed all the help it could get.

Time for the *limpieza*, or cleansing.

I pulled out the piece of paper Lorena had included with the kit containing phrases in Yoruba, the West African language of Lucumí or Santería. Taking a deep breath, I began with regular words of my own.

"I ask the Universe to cleanse and bless this home, fill it with light and love, remove all negative energy that is not welcome here."

Spreading the sage, I wandered through the house, paying particular attention to the corners where negative energy was said to build up. Then I came back to my starting point and glanced at Maggie's instructions.

Perform when not on your period and while smoking a cigar.

Well, I wasn't on my period, that much I knew. And a cigar? Shit, I hadn't smoked one of those since I was fifteen at my *quince* birthday party, when Abuelo made me try one for his own amusement. Looking through the bag, I noticed they hadn't included one.

Ugh, fail.

As weird as it seemed, this was an important part of the ritual to those who practiced, and I didn't feel right skipping it. But I knew, if I walked around the house, I was sure to find one, as Dr. Rivera, like most elderly Cuban men, kept a stash of cigars somewhere in the house. I was sure he wouldn't miss one if I borrowed it.

"Where are you suckers?" I walked through the living room, opening and closing random trinket boxes. If I was a random cigar, where would I be? The lid of one trinket box was upholstered in leather and smelled sweetly of tobacco. Opening it, I found it contained an assortment of cigars.

"BINGO."

Finding a cigar in a home decked out in Cuban décor had proved easy. Next, I checked to make sure nobody was watching me steal, nobody alive anyway. I swiped a box of matches from inside the box and a cigar from the bottom of the stack before returning to my spot.

"Alright, I'm ready now," I said to myself, lighting the cigar and puffing on the end until it glowed orange. I coughed, feeling a burn in my throat, coughed again. My eyes stung with smoke. "Amateur," I muttered.

As I'd done with Wiccan spells over the years, I tried to take it seriously and focus on my intention to rid the house of spirits. The magic wasn't in the items themselves—it was in the practitioner who believed they could manifest change.

Opening the back French doors as well as the front, I returned to the mop and bucket and, as quickly as possible, began mopping the tile floors while repeating the words on the piece of paper.

"Elegua, abreme camino, librame de mal," I said in Spanish then switched to the Yoruba on my paper. *"Eshu Elegua, oga gbogbo na mirin ita algbana baba mi mulo na buruku nitosi le chocncho kuelu kuikuo oki cosi ofo, cosi eyo..."*

I had no idea what I was saying, but I tried to infuse the same feeling I'd used with the English phrases. Intention, intention, intention. What did I want to achieve? I envisioned myself achieving a clean house, spirits moving away, peace being restored. I mopped the floors, the idea being to usher the negative spirits toward the door, to "sweep them out."

When I was done, I returned to my bag, pulled out a white candle, set it on a small plate, and lit it in the middle of the coffee table.

"Ashes to ashes, dust to dust," I said after a long exhale, "may the wind blow all wandering spirits, clear the world of the living, turn you to where you belong, and—"

Something fell.

I startled, touched my chest.

My eyes flicked around. Through the cigar smoke, I spotted something lying on the floor. A photo frame. Slowly, I walked over to pick it up. The photo was a faded color image of Dr. Rivera next to—now this part was a challenge—either Mrs. Rivera in her younger, healthier years (but that would've made her much, much younger than Dr. Rivera) or…they had a daughter. Either way, I could see the familial resemblance. Whoever the gorgeous woman was, she smiled joyfully and cradled a baby bump.

I put the frame back.

The room felt chilly, though the doors were open and warm South Florida air wafted through the house. Someone was here with me—someone from the spirit world.

They didn't want to go, just like Bibi had said.

But I wouldn't back down.

I had to make them leave.

"Eshu Elegua, oga gbogbo na mirin ita algbana baba mi mulo na buruku nitosi le chocncho kuelu kuikuo oki cosi ofo, cosi eyo…"

I read from the paper, repeating the chant, picking up the smudge stick and dipping it into the white candle flame again. Spreading the sweet sage smoke through the air, I envisioned the spirits leaving out the front door, even the one who hadn't liked the framed photo and knocked it over.

But my confidence waned. If a ghost was sticking around, then I wasn't doing a good job. And if I didn't believe in my powers, my powers wouldn't work.

"Please leave," I ordered the lingering spirit. "There's nothing left here for you. It's time to move on."

Suddenly, the living room walls reverberated with the sound of pounding. Whoever was here in spirit had not liked what I had to say. I gasped, clutching my wrist and lucky bracelet.

"You'll be happier if you go," I insisted, heart pounding. "Trust me…let it go."

Another shadow slipped in my peripheral vision, but when I faced it head-on, nothing was there. I closed the doors, grabbed the bucket containing spell water, and headed for the stairs, desperate to get the hell out of this creepy-ass room.

At the base of the stairs, I paused.

It was that music again.

The old-style 1950s music that sounded like it was playing on a vintage record player. It might've been coming from the dining room. Putting down the bucket and bag, I tip-toed down the hallway into the dining hall only to find it empty, yet the music felt discernibly louder.

Where was it coming from? Like the phantom cries in the garden, the notes were difficult to pinpoint.

More importantly, I felt obsessed with it. Slipping out the same door I'd found on my first visit, I found myself inside that empty ballroom, the one that, in my mind's eye, could've hosted dignitaries and millionaires from all over the country in Julia Harding's time.

I walked all along the perimeter of its walls, trying to see if there was another door to another room only to find myself on the opposite side of the house in a long, dark hallway that turned like a hairpin at the end.

I swallowed a lump in my throat.

Good Lord, I couldn't go down that path. It felt musty in here, disconnected from the home's main A/C, like an annexed, unused area—a ramp descending into Hell. I had no idea where it led and wasn't sure I wanted to know. But the music was louder here, and I felt like I was onto something.

Opportunities like this didn't present themselves often, and the gothic girl in me couldn't resist. And so I walked. Slowly. Down the hallway. Following the music like a guest in a mad scientist's castle out of some old Hollywood monster movie.

I touched the walls on both sides as I went, feeling off-balance before realizing that the hallway was leading down. It was hard to tell because the corridor was so long, and the descent was gradual but when I reached the end and slowly turned the corner of the wall to see where the hairpin turn led, I noticed another hallway descending the rest of the way.

The music grew louder.

This was the cellar—it had to be.

But Dr. Rivera had said it'd been closed years ago after Hurricane Andrew. I picked up speed and let gravity and momentum carry me down the ramp until I reached the bottom where a pocket of cold air greeted me.

But no door was there. I'd reached a dead-end. I ran my fingertips along the walls, trying to feel inconsistencies in the murkiness and did come across a different texture. A rough patch-up job. New drywall, new-smelling materials. New addition. The cellar had been sealed after all.

But the music came from inside.

At least, it seemed to.

I turned back the way I came before someone might find me down here when suddenly, I stopped frozen still in the ramped hallway. A figure stood in my path—a woman in a pale blue dress, gaunt, with thin hair pulled into a messy ponytail, bleeding from the chest and a large chunk of skin missing from her collarbone. Her knees knocked together, and she popped her chin up and stared at me.

Imploring, angry eyes.

How can you not help me, she said without a word. *How can you stand there and do nothing? Especially in your condition?*

This time, I screamed my head off.

ELEVEN

I wedged my way past her, squeezing my eyes shut, pretending she wasn't there. I pushed my body against the wall. As if she were real and needed space in the hall. As if she were made of flesh and bone. Screams echoed in my ear—her screams. She was one pissed-off woman. But she couldn't be real. There was no way a person looking so dead could possibly be so alive.

"Okay, I'm sorry, I'm sorry..." I reasoned with the woman, trying to get past.

The chill in the hall intensified, as I blasted past the ghost and up the ramp with blinders on, my hands shielding the sides of my face, as if doing so would make her disappear.

How can you go?

How can you let me die?

"I didn't. I'm not," I assured her.

I rushed around the hairpin turn and up the long hallway toward the entrance into the main house. Her bloody features would be imprinted in my memory as long as I lived. I could hear her moaning behind me, groaning about how nobody would help her.

"Get out, get out, get out..." I chanted to myself, still ridiculously using my hands as blinders. All I had to do was reach the lit doorway and I'd be free from this hellish hall way. Why? Why did I have to come this way? Why did I have to "investigate?" I was a glutton for punishment, that's why. I'd led such a boring life so far that I needed drama.

Needed bloody, screaming ghosts in order to feel alive. The scary thing was, it wasn't too far from the truth.

But then, because Life decided it was time for me to learn my lesson the full-immersion way, my body smacked right into another solid body smelling of cigar and old man cologne.

"Oh, my God! I'm so sorry," I panted.

"*¿Qué haces aquí, muchacha?*" the old man asked with a stern look in his eye. "You're not supposed to be here."

"I did? No, I didn't. I mean…who…who is that woman down there?" I pointed down the shadowy hallway.

"What are you looking for?" He ignored my question.

"I heard music and…followed… I thought maybe…the cellar…who was…?"

God, I sounded like a bumbling idiot, and Dr. Rivera took full advantage to glare at me like one. Then, he glanced at my white pants' pocket and cocked his head.

"*¿Qué'eso?*" He forcefully stepped toward me, wanting to know what was in my pocket.

Instinctively, I backed away. After the ghost woman in the hall, I couldn't be sure that he wasn't after me, too. But he only grabbed my arm and pulled me toward him, so he could fish into my pocket. "Where did you get this?" He raised the cigar I'd borrowed from his box.

Oh. That.

"I was going to put that back. I needed a cigar for the *limpieza* and forgot one at home. I'm so sorry, I—"

Was an idiot.

"So, you thought..." The old man's eyes took on a menacing look mixed with disbelieving amusement, as he held up the cigar. "That you'd borrow my Montecristo, No. 2, of all the cigars you could have chosen in that box...for...let me get this straight...a *despojo*?"

He scoffed.

"I didn't know—"

"Let me guess, you'd like some of my best rum to go with that, too? Come, I'll show you where my most expensive flask is."

"No, sir. I didn't know that was one of your best cigars. I'm so sorry. I'm going to go now. Clearly, I haven't been the best person for this job."

What had I been thinking? I couldn't have botched this up any worse, and who was I kidding? I couldn't deal with that ghost in the pale blue dress and bent knees either. I was unequivocally, undeniably unqualified.

"I can't believe this," Dr. Rivera laughed. That was an improvement. At least he had a sense of humor, assuming it was a real laugh and not one of those mad-scientist maniacal ones that comes right before a person loses their shit on you. "Do you know why I went to your store, Quey*lín*?"

"Because you needed help."

"Because I needed someone *reliable*, someone intelligent. Someone who had studied religions and the metaphysical relationships between them. Real religion, not esoteric pseudo *mierda*. For Santería, I would've gone to Calle Ocho or Hialeah."

Damn. Don't hold back, old man.

"So, I'm guessing you don't believe it works?"

"It's voodoo," he snapped, shaking the cigar for emphasis. "I thought you were finer than that. I never imagined a store owner from Coconut Grove would smoke a cigar and wash my floors with Rompe Saraguey. *Qué verguenza.*" He shook his head of perfect white hair disappointedly.

"And yet, you know what Rompe Saraguey is," I said, my voice full of tone. You know the one. The one that made patriarchs arch their eyebrows at you.

I shouldn't have. Not now, not after I'd stolen his best cigar and lit it to do what he considered to be an uneducated country bumpkin's religion.

"Of course, I do. Anybody who has studied does."

"Okay, then," I said, out of breath. So far, this day had taken a lot out of me. "I'm sorry I took your cigar. And I'm sorry I tried to help you without getting the full scope of your religious views first. My mistake."

I headed back to the hallway to get my things. I didn't need this shit. I'd only tried to help the man and sure, make a few bucks, too. Oh, yes, and gain myself some paranormal experience. Well, I definitely got that.

"Quey*lín,*" he said softly.

I paused to look at him.

"I'm sorry. I didn't mean to offend you. I don't have anything against Santería, if that's what you believe. I just...I don't believe. I thought you'd be working with God."

"Why not call an exorcist, Dr. Rivera? If God is what you believe in, and the Devil is what you fear?"

He didn't answer.

We stood looking at each other. I'd disappointed him, but to be fair, he never asked exactly how I'd be performing my task, and besides, Santería wasn't the only form of spellcraft I used today. I'd also talked to the Universe, called upon the elements, and spoke directly with the spirits.

If my shop, if my own beliefs were anything, they were eclectic.

"There's no cellar," he simply said. "I told you that already. You can go anywhere in the house. Use whatever method you think is best. I apologize. Just, please…stay away from here."

He brushed past me, clearing his throat.

I headed toward the foot of the stairs to grab the bucket and my things. Even though he seemed fine with me staying, I wasn't sure I wanted to anymore. Yes, the money would be nice, but I didn't need shame stamped onto my forehead. I didn't need to upset this man with my methods either, and I sure as hell didn't need the old-fashioned guilt.

At the door to the dining room, he looked at me again. "Careful what you look for, *niña*. You just might find it."

By the bay, I sat on the cement dock, knees drawn to my chest. I was still shaking, even an hour later. If I smoked, this would the moment I'd light a cigarette to calm my nerves. Maybe take a hit of weed. But I'd never indulged in either, so all I could do was meditate.

I focused on the water, on the sparkling surface of the beautiful blue ocean. On the warm breezes and the swaying palm trees. As peaceful as these grounds were, I couldn't escape everything that had just happened inside that house.

For thirty years, I'd managed to never see a single ghost, and now in one day, I'd seen several moving shadows, a photo frame fall off a shelf by itself, and two full-bodied apparitions, both of them ghastly as hell.

It was confirmed—the Harding Estate was haunted. Also of notable assessment? I was ineffective as a medium.

I sighed.

I closed my eyes, breathing in and out, doing my best to calm my nerves. "Spirit guides, tell me what I should do," I spoke quietly into the air.

I'd never actually seen my spirit guides, so why did I continue to talk to them? Why couldn't I do the same with God before I'd decided to explore other spiritual options?

"Do I leave or stay until I've finished?" I asked the silence.

I still had the upstairs to clean and then I'd hoped to do a final spell on the whole house from the outside, but what would be the point? Other than getting paid?

So many questions burned at me. Like, where had that ethereal music come from? Had it been real or from another realm? Who was the woman in the pale blue dress? Why had she been missing a chunk of skin? Was she really talking to me or someone else?

Explanations flowed through my mind like binary code on a computer screen, not a single one helpful for getting the job done. Maybe the female ghost had been hit by a car and died nearby. Maybe she'd died in a boating accident off the shore. Maybe she'd died in the house.

Who knew? It wasn't important for me to figure out who the ghosts were. Doing so could take forever, and Dr. and Mrs. Rivera only wanted them gone. I understood why Bibi left this morning.

It was too much for anyone.

I pulled my phone from my bag to check in with her and noticed several missed calls and texts from Samuel and Maggie, both asking if I was okay.

I replied to Sam first, telling him that yes, while everything was okay, I was rattled at the moment, though dealing with it. At that moment, a call came in from the store.

"Hello." My voice sounded distant and haggard.

"Queylin, it's Maggie. How are you, hon? How's it going?"

"Not that well."

"Why, what's going on?"

"I'll tell you about it when I leave, but basically, I have a lot to learn."

"It was too much for you then?"

"You could say that. How's Bibi? She didn't look too good when she left here. She seemed eager to get back to *Goddess Moon*."

"What do you mean? Bibi hasn't come in. I thought she was with you."

I sat up straight. "She's not. She left early and said she'd be at the store by noon." Alarm bells went off in my head, as I tried to remember everything Bibi had told me this morning, though she hadn't spoken much. I was fairly certain she said she'd be going back to work, though.

I needed to contact her right away. "Hey, let me call you back."

"Yep. Let me know if you find her."

"I will."

"And Queylin?"

"Yup."

"Be careful, hon. I don't know why, but I'm getting past life vibes from inside the house. I don't think you were ever Julia Harding in the past, but you're very connected to her for some reason. I just read that she killed herself."

"I got that impression, too."

"Okay. So if you feel at all like you're in danger, get out. Got it?"

"I will. Thanks, Maggie." I hung up and immediately called Bibi, but the call went to voicemail. I texted her instead.

Hey, you OK?

The text was delivered, but no reply. A million scenarios blew through my mind, not a single one being rational. Maybe she'd been in a car crash. Maybe she'd fallen ill and headed straight for the doctor. Maybe she took the long way and wandered into another creepy house at the behest of her former babysitter turned employer.

I couldn't contain my worry, though I knew it was irrational. Finally, after a minute of staring at my phone and listening to seagulls soothe my mind, the bubbles of imminent reply showed up on the screen.

I'm OK, she said. *Felt sick. Went home to rest.*

Didn't know. Maggie was waiting for you, I replied.

Sorry. I should've called her. Headache. Bye.

I sent her a Bitmoji of myself doing yoga, hoping to cheer her up, but no stickers came back.

Still, it was a huge load off my mind knowing she was fine, though I'd hoped to tell her what happened to me then ask her for advice. But Bibi wanted nothing more to do with this house, so it wouldn't be right to bother her anymore.

I was about to call Maggie and ask what she thought I should do—stay or go—when I thought I saw something.

Someone standing far away directly in front of the back patio. I had to squint to make sure I wasn't seeing things.

Long period dress. Hair pinned into a loose chignon at the top of her head, hands cradled around her belly. Watching me.

Wearing *white*.

The more I stared at the female figure, the more I realized she wasn't looking at me at all, but watching the horizon, waiting nervously, full of anguish, for someone to arrive. I followed her line of sight toward the water, as though I could see what she stared at.

A boat.

Yes, she was waiting for someone to arrive.

Then I got that odd thought again. The one where I felt like the love of my life would never return. It wasn't a fear about my own husband, I now realized. It was about another man. A man Julia waited for, day in, day out. It wasn't my own thought at all, but belonging to the woman I was staring at.

If I closed my eyes and focused hard enough, I could almost hear the man's name, the man on her mind. But one thing was for sure—it wasn't her husband. It wasn't the same man who'd put her in this house and forgotten about her. It was the man she'd hoped would steal her away.

A man who would never come.

The man she'd hung herself out by that tree for, knowing it was the only way she'd ever be reunited with him. The father of her unborn child.

TWELVE

I wiped my eyes.

How did I know all that? Where was this information coming from? Yes, I'd always felt connected to that tree in the garden, but being near it was doing something to me. I wasn't sure how to react. I only knew that Dr. Rivera was right—I should be careful what I looked for, I just might find it.

Walking up the broken flagstones toward the house, I stared at the banyan. The roots dropping from the branches made it look as though the tree were melting. Memories of Julia hanging from the tree still freaked me out. She'd used one of the hanging roots as rope. It'd been so easy—too easy—to tie one into a noose and...

I shook off the vision.

Heading up the path to the spot where I'd seen Julia a moment ago, I was determined to try and do good. To communicate. She had appeared to me for a reason, and I'd finally seen a spirit. I had to try and help. When I reached the gravel walkway a few feet in front of the back patio, however, I stopped and tried to find her. I searched the grounds.

I waited, taking in the silence.

The unsettling silence.

She did not materialize again.

"Julia, I'm sorry for whatever happened to you," I said, my whispers carrying on the ocean breeze. Birds' chirping and bugs' buzzing filled in the stillness. "I saw you waiting for a loved one. Whoever he was, he must've been special."

No voices, no words.

Only the rustling of palm fronds.

"But you should probably leave now. You'll be happier if you do. He's not here. In fact, I'm willing to bet he's waiting for you on the other side."

My body tensed, as I braced for another attack, just in case she didn't like what I had to say and wanted to run me over again. My arms crossed over my breasts which still felt sore when I stopped to think about it. After a few minutes of trying to feel her energy, I gave up and went inside.

I had to finish what I started, get my check, and say goodbye to Dr. Rivera. This whole experience had been...eye-opening, to say the least. Grabbing the bucket and my bag, I headed for the stairs, determined to complete the *limpieza* when the bucket fell from my hands.

Or rather, was *knocked* from my hands.

It toppled over and the water spilled all over the veranda.

"Shit."

I didn't have more of the enchanted herb solution, so I'd have to finish with nothing but intention. A good witch could make anything happen, even without "ingredients." The items were only there to guide your thoughts toward your intention.

Reaching the top of the stairs, I asked for guidance, love and light from the universe, and then I filled the halls with the sweet scent of burned white sage while asking for protection. The protection part was especially important after what I'd seen in the hallway leading to the site of the former cellar.

Dr. Rivera might've insisted that no cellar existed, but I wasn't so sure. It was there, and though that hallway had led to a sealed wall, I knew I'd heard music playing on the other side. The pale dress ghost guarding the sealed wall knew it, too.

As I mopped the floors with what little was left of the special herb blend and read aloud the African incantation, I focused on the woman in the pale blue dress. She had asked for help, wanted to know why no one would assist her, and I would do my best to address her specifically.

"Universe, please help Julia, the woman from my dream last night, and the woman in the downstairs hallway," I said, calling them to the forefront of my memory. "Please help them find peace from this realm. Please help them find closure."

And then I realized.

They were probably here for that reason—because they hadn't found closure to their pain. No amount of inexperienced Santería, prayer, or pleading on my part would change that, or they would've left already. Anything I was hoping to accomplish was for simple hauntings, for ghosts who couldn't find their way. But this house required aggressive action, forcing them to leave.

I mopped the guest bedroom with the mop which was getting dry now, keeping an eye out for the woman holding the jewelry. I also mopped a mostly empty room containing a large display case filled with bath towels and linens, and two other bedrooms containing dated furniture, simple shelves, and no artwork. As I finished up in the hallway, though, I caught a scent.

Something cooking.

It could've been soup, chicken, stew, or any number of dishes, but I couldn't pinpoint exactly which. Then again, if Lovely did most of the cooking in this house, I wasn't familiar with many Haitian meals to recognize which. I had to say, though, it wasn't a very appetizing scent.

In fact, it countered every pleasant scent I had mopped onto the floors, undoing the positive energy I was working so hard to lay down.

As I entered the guest bedroom to change out of my sweaty clothes, I heard a soft sound coming down the hallway. Terrified of seeing the woman in the blue dress again, or the woman from my dream, I returned to the hall cautiously, focusing on the floor in case an apparition awaited me. Slowly, I looked up. Nobody was there. I timidly checked the opposite end and didn't see anyone there either. But I still heard the sound.

Crying.

Someone was sniffling again, quietly sobbing in private. A woman's cries. It could've been Lovely or Barbara Rivera, but if it was Lovely, then someone else had to be cooking. Only I realized then that I couldn't smell the food anymore. Either I'd gotten used to it quickly or the scent had dissipated.

Or...

The smell had never been here to begin with. Not today anyway. A phantom smell from another time.

Sneaking quietly, I followed the sound of crying to the end of the hall, to the room with the closed door. I'd avoided this room earlier figuring it was the master bedroom. Though it probably needed a good clearing more than any other space in the house, I hadn't wanted to intrude on anyone's privacy. Now, I noticed the door was slightly ajar.

The crying grew louder, as I got closer.

It was definitely coming from inside.

The hairs on my arms stood on end.

"Hello?" I called softly.

At the door, I leaned my ear. Someone was definitely inside the room sobbing their heart out. I shouldn't have been eavesdropping. I should've respected their space and walked away, except I needed to know if they were okay. Given the fact that the women in this house had not uttered a word in my presence, I needed to know if they were in need of help.

"Please, are you okay? I want to help."

The crying stopped.

Ever so slightly, I pushed the door open an inch at a time, analyzing each item that came into view in order of appearance—an ornate dresser, a wicker laundry basket in the corner, more gorgeous art of nude women, the edge of the bed draped by a white macramé coverlet. When I caught sight of metal and rubber, I stopped.

Mrs. Rivera's wheelchair.

Here was this woman who hadn't spoken a word to me since I'd arrived, who the doctor had insisted had degenerated, yet she cried as though her pain were fresh. I felt so incredibly sad for her and wanted to offer sympathy, if I could.

"Mrs. Rivera?" I took one step into the room, just far enough so I could look past the wall leading into the master bedroom, so she could see me as well.

Her chair was parked in front of a large floor-to-ceiling window covered in gauzy white curtains. The sunlight filtered through them, casting soft shadows throughout the elegant room. The old woman stared outside, gripping her armrests like she always did. Her large yellow sunhat belied the lack of energy she displayed.

"I'm sorry for interrupting," I said quietly. "I just wanted to make sure you were okay. I heard you crying."

I stood there a minute, hoping for a response. Now that she was alone, maybe she'd feel safe enough to open up to me, tell me more about what was going on. So far, I'd gotten her husband's point of view, but I was sure there was more to hers, if only she would speak to me.

But Mrs. Rivera wouldn't acknowledge me. I'd caught her in a private moment, and now I felt ashamed.

"I'm sorry, I'll go—"

From the other side of the wall, a shadowy silhouette came at me, placing itself between my view of Mrs. Rivera and the sunlit curtains, creating a dark shape, scaring the shit out of me in the process. My heart nearly stopped until I realized it was Lovely, the housekeeper, ushering me out of the room with aggressive haste.

Her hands waved me away, her eyes pleaded with terror for me to leave. As if she feared what might happen if the old man of the house were to find out I had stepped into this room or attempted to speak to his wife outside of his presence. As though my being here had triggered a momentary lapse in security.

"I'm sorry." I backed out of the room, as Lovely pushed me out. Her fingers jabbed at me to go, go, go. "I was only checking on Mrs. Rivera. Is she alright?"

But catching sight of Lovely's face in the brightness of the hallway made me wonder if I'd been wrong about so many things. Her eyes were tinged with redness, two glistening patches of skin underneath them. I wish I could say her tear-filled eyes were the most prominent thing about her face in full daylight, but they weren't.

Her mouth was.

Seeing Lovely up-close for the first time, I was able to notice that her lips wouldn't part. They seemed almost fused together, as though the line that divided most lips wasn't even there. It was probably a trick of the light, but considering I'd never heard her speak either, something inside me crushed the air out of my lungs.

"Was that you?" I asked, stepping back, my eyes riveted on her mouth. "Was that you crying? Do you need help? Should I bring the police here?" I whispered the last words. This was my one chance to help her if I could. Soon, I'd be gone and back to my world.

Why I felt like she needed assistance was beyond me, but I was grasping at straws, trying to guess what her heart needed but her lips couldn't tell me.

Lovely's dark eyes widened with dread.

No, she seemed to say. *Whatever you do, please don't do that.*

Suddenly, she opened a hallway closet filled with knickknacks and boxes and pulled something out of the corner. It was long and tall, a dark pole, like those African rain sticks my elementary school music teachers used to pass around and let us play with, only longer.

Her face took on a determined expression just then, so deep, I thought maybe she was going to hit me with the stick, but she grabbed it with both hands, and with fierce determination, struck the wooden floor.

I couldn't help but notice that she actually marked the old wood, and I didn't know how Dr. Rivera would feel about that, but if this was my house, I would've scolded her for marking the floor.

Apparently, she didn't care and struck the floor again. And again.

All the while, her eyes grew wilder and focused on me. Her breathing intensified through her nose, as her nostrils flared, a result of not being able to open her mouth. But this didn't impede her from humming, and she droned out a tune, something like an old folk song, something that sounded vaguely familiar.

Last night.

I'd heard it last night as I was trying to fall asleep with Bibi.

Lovely struck the floor again, closed her eyes, and raised her free hand to the ceiling. Her sandaled feet shuffled in tune to her song, and I felt caught up in a dream. I watched with fascination as one hand clutched the handrail.

It wasn't strange to see a Haitian woman engaged in what seemed to be a ritualistic dance of some kind. Many people in my city hailed from Caribbean islands, from cultures derived from slavery, from West African nations before that. Their religions morphed into Santería in Cuba and Puerto Rico and *Vodou* in Haiti. Plus, I got the sense that, having seen me mop the floors earlier while smoking a cigar, Lovely felt comfortable showing me that she, too, followed a secret religion.

None of that was strange.

What was strange was the mist that appeared in the middle of the bedroom opposite the master. A gray haze that took form into the shape of a man. The particles swirled and coalesced, as my legs weakened, and my knees touched the floor, and I couldn't believe what I was seeing, because only two days ago, I hadn't had this ability.

All I could do was watch in awe.

The well-built, dark-skinned man stood in the middle of the room before my eyes, and I knew that Lovely had summoned *un muerto*—a dead person, a spirit—and something told me, from the way he stood comfortably, to the sun-faded pants he wore, to the amber stains on his shirt and the yellowed captain's hat, that this was someone who had appeared in this bedroom quite often.

His hands reached out, implored me. His mouth opened. He spoke, but I couldn't hear him. It was as if we lived on different radio frequencies, but I felt his desperation, knew he wanted me to give someone a message. That he loved her. That he'd been on his way back before he'd been intercepted, shot at sea.

Tell her, please.

Tell her Roger is waiting.

THIRTEEN

Julia's man.

The lover she cried over while wandering the grounds of her stately home, the man she waited for by the ocean. The father of her unborn child.

Roger.

No wonder Julia Harding had hung herself. Not only was she pregnant by a man not her husband based on the visions I'd had, but they'd been a biracial couple in the 20s in a country rife with racism.

Roger appeared as a gray mist that gave off a cold energy, freezing my body from the outside in, until my core was shaking. One second, his outline and features were clear—tall, muscular, handsome. The next, he swirled with the mist and appeared as a cloud. It felt like a dream, and I knew I would question what I'd seen later on.

"I'll tell her," I muttered, as my midsection ached with soreness. I winced and wrapped my cold arms full of goose bumps around myself. "You can go. You're free."

Just leave, I told him without words.

But I wasn't sure Roger could hear me, even though I could "hear" him, though no words were spoken aloud. I heard his message as a "knowing." I didn't like a feeling I got from his presence, though, as if he hadn't gone peacefully from this world. As if he'd been tortured or drowned.

Roger wasn't one of the resident ghosts at the Harding Estate, though. If he were, Lovely wouldn't have had to summon him with her *muerto* stick. His spirit had traveled through time and space to get here. His was a soul that had moved on without regrets, called back to Earth as an ancestor. His message had been for Julia to join him.

The cramps that interrupted the visit just then felt so real, so corporeal, I couldn't tell if they were mine or Julia's. My face lowered to the floor, touching the mopped, wooden floorboards to ease the pain. I couldn't see Roger from this position anymore, yet I knew he had gone. A veil of energy lifted off the hallway, just as an obscure tunnel closed in around my vision.

Make it stop, make it stop…

I closed my eyes and was gone.

I'd been hit by a bus.

Attacked by linebackers.

Squished in a human panini press.

That was how I felt—ample soreness, dull aches, and sharp pains all over my body. My collarbone and breasts hurt more than they had yesterday after Julia's ghost had slammed into me. Opening my eyes a little at a time, I saw I was lying in bed, but couldn't tell what time of day it was.

Or where I was.

Someone touched my arm, waking me from a prolonged alpha state. I saw the housekeeper, or nurse, medicine woman, or whoever Lovely really was, setting down a glass of water on the nightstand. She gave me a worried glance and felt my forehead for fever. I was grateful for the attention and thought of my mother somewhere in the city, assuming her daughter was fine. Little did she know what I was up to.

I blinked and tried to smile at Lovely, but then I saw through her body, laid over her body, connected to her same aura was the woman who'd haunted this room last night. A clear overlay of the dead on top of the living.

God, no.

Too many ghosts.

I'd heard of people who suddenly became psychic after traumatic events, such as the death of a loved one, or a car accident. But I'd never heard of anyone becoming psychic after getting hit by an angry spirit, though. Or from spending time in a haunted home. I'd spent plenty of time at haunted hotels in my life, hoping to catch a glimpse of the supernatural, but nothing like this had ever happened.

It made sense, though.

But it might've been a dream.

Dreams and reality blended at Harding Estate.

When I opened my eyes, the mystery woman was still there, only now she'd moved out of Lovely and sat in the corner of the room, dirty knees drawn to her chest, nervously chewing on her fingertips. Lovely had gone from the room, and now it was just me and this woman.

I sat up to make sure the vision was real and not a lucid dream.

Aside from being a ghost, there was nothing terrifying about the woman. Not like the lady in the pale blue dress with her screams and bleeding wounds. No, this lady projected sadness. She desperately wanted to say something but couldn't. As if she'd long forgotten what she felt sorrow for.

111

When I blinked, she was gone from the corner. Then something shuffled above me. I looked up and saw she had moved. Now, she sat, cross-legged, upside-down on the ceiling staring down at me like Charlotte dangling from her web. I didn't care if she was harmless, I'd reached my ghostly vision quota for the day and bolted from the room.

Barefoot and confused, the smell of cooked meat returned to my consciousness. Burning flesh. Now, the scents coming from downstairs were infinitely better, provoking my empty stomach. Herbs, and vegetables, and foods meant for consumption. I glanced nervously into the guest room again to see if she was still watching me.

Empty.

Heading downstairs, I followed the light sounds of silverware to the dining room where Dr. Rivera was seated alone, drinking soup with a glass of wine.

"Ah, there she is." He said this using a grand gesture with his hand and another charming smile to welcome me.

I wasn't having his formalities anymore. More than charm, I needed to know what was going on. "What happened?"

"You fainted."

"How do you know I fainted?" I asked. "You weren't there."

"Lovely told me."

"Lovely doesn't speak," I said.

The doctor sighed and set down his spoon to rest against the inside of the bowl. "She came to find me, Quey*lín*. She speaks, just not with words. We lifted and carried you to the bed. *¿Te sientes mejor?* You slept quite a bit. Here, sit, so you can eat."

I had, in fact, slept quite a bit. In fact, the sun was low in the sky, judging from the darkness in the house.

As much as I wanted to decline the meal or any other courtesies the good doctor might've extended, I was starving for something to eat. Dehydrated, too. Apparently, all this sudden psychic ability had made my throat parched.

I sat on the edge of a dining chair without committing to full posture, poured myself a glass of water from a glass decanter, and chugged the whole thing down in one, long chug.

"God, I feel so sick," I mumbled.

"Yes, you don't look too well. Maybe you have *fiebre*."

He might've been right—I did feel feverish.

"Where's Mrs. Rivera?" I asked, looking in the usual places—the windows, the veranda outside. "Haven't seen her around much."

"She wasn't feeling well either."

"Why is that?"

"What do you mean?"

"Why doesn't she talk? Your wife. Or move?"

I know I sounded curt, but I wasn't in the most polite of moods, especially after the way he'd spoken to me earlier after I'd discovered the ramp leading down into the non-cellar.

Dr. Rivera studied me a moment before resuming his soup. "I told you, she suffers from many mental disorders. But I'm glad you bring this up, Quey*lín*. Since you are so curious about my wife, about the *cellar* that doesn't exist anymore, and other things on the property, I thought I might tell you a few facts about the things that walk here at night."

"Not just at night," I added. "They're everywhere. At all times of the day."

"So you have seen them."

"I have."

"Did you ask them to leave with your *brujería*?" He chuckled.

"I did."

I watched as he took two more spoonfuls of soup then wiped his mouth with a cloth napkin and set it down across his lap again.

"I'm sure you've seen Julia. She's the one who haunts the outside of the house, the one most psychics see. Though my wife has seen her inside the house from time to time, always confused and searching for someone."

Probably her lover, I thought.

"Yes, I've seen her." Julia Harding's ghost seemed to have a one-track mind, being reunited with Roger and little else. Then again, it was my understanding that most earthbound ghosts were obsessed with something, else they'd move on.

"Well, she died in 1921 near the beginning of Prohibition, and it's believed she was pregnant when she passed."

"She was," I blurted. "At least that's the impression I've gotten from her."

He stared at me, and a slow smile unfurled on his face. "Yes, that makes sense."

"What does?" I raised an eyebrow.

"Psychics over the years have all reported an angry woman in white, *La Dama de Blanco*, as you already know. But for a while, they didn't know she was pregnant. It was interesting how they figured it out."

"How?"

The king looked around at his castle. "This house has an unfortunate history with pregnancy. Any child born here dies shortly after. Other pregnancies have ended as stillborn or miscarriages. It seems Julia is curious of pregnant women. Envious, too. A couple of the mediums over the years were expecting, and she gave them the hardest of times. That's why no family has occupied this home for very long."

"You're saying she cursed the house from ever having kids live in it?"

"Well, I don't know if I believe in curses," he said. "But I do in coincidences. And the screams we hear in the night, I believe those are screams of childbirth from another time. Of loss and pain. I believe ghosts are past traumas, energies imprinted in a home."

And I believed ghosts were the souls of people who endured those traumas. Either way, the atmosphere in these spots was tainted.

Like the horrible cramps and soreness I'd had all day, especially after I fainted. If I was picking up Julia's emotions, it made sense that I was also picking up her physical sensations as well. Ghosts, energies, imprints. All residue of past lives.

"That's horrible," I said. "This house has a sad, negative energy about it. I never noticed it as a teen when I trespassed here. Then again, I never came inside. But now..."

"Now it's different."

"Why?" I asked.

"You are different than when you were a teen, Quey*lin*. Didn't you have experiences last night and today? I do recall you running up the ramp terrified."

"Well, yes. But what about you? You don't consider yourself psychic, yet you called me here because you claim to hear ghosts at night."

"My wife hears and sees them," he clarified. "I don't see them."

"Not even a little? You don't feel them?"

"No. I am doing this for her. Why does she hear them and not me?" he asked.

I searched my mind for an explanation. "Everyone has different sensitivities. When your brain is at rest, like when you're sleeping, you're more likely to tune into that frequency than you are during the day. Which is why many people report seeing ghosts in the middle of the night."

"Or, they could be dreaming." He smiled facetiously. "The brain is powerful, Quey*lín*."

If he wasn't sure that ghosts prowled his house at night, then why had he invited me here? You wouldn't expect the person who hired the medium to be the skeptic. There was more to my being here.

But I wouldn't argue anymore. People like Dr. Rivera, living as recluses, craved conversation. He was engaging me in a discussion just to have someone to talk to. I knew ghosts were real and not a manifestation of our own imaginations or overactive brains. Granted, they *could* be hallucinations, but not always. Why would my mind conjure up four different spirits all in the same day inside the same reputably haunted house?

"There's something else I should tell you," Dr. Rivera said, reaching for his glass of wine. He took another sip then set it down again. "My wife lost our child fifteen years ago. When we first moved into this house."

"Oh, I'm sorry." I hadn't expected this to be his confession. Now I understood the connection, why he thought there might be a curse.

I imagined Mrs. Rivera in her catatonic state, reliving her loss fifteen years ago. I could see how losing something so meaningful could ruin your mental wellbeing for life, how it could age you significantly, too.

But wasn't Dr. Rivera too old to be a new father? Suddenly, I thought of the photo in the living room, the one that had been knocked down during the cleansing. I'd thought the woman had been his daughter.

Was Mrs. Rivera a much younger wife?

He picked up his napkin to dab his eyes. "She went into early labor at twenty-six weeks. The fetus was too weak to survive. Help did not arrive on time. The baby died here. In this house."

"Oh."

"I'm sure now you're thinking this place is beyond help," he laughed, taking another sip of his wine. He wiped his lips and folded his hands in his lap, thick fingers interlaced. "That's what the other mediums believed. But I tell you all this, to be fair."

"To be fair?"

"Yes. I didn't know this when I invited you here, but...well...you're pregnant, too."

FOURTEEN

"I'm sorry…what?"

I stared at the old man. Why would he say something like that? How would even *know* unless he was psychic himself?

"Well, you are, aren't you?"

"Are you asking me, or telling me? I don't know. I…" I stammered. I mean, I hadn't really thought about it. Samuel and I weren't exactly being careful, but we weren't actively planning a child either.

"*Ay, Diós.*" He pinched the bridge of his nose. "I didn't mean to upset you. I thought you knew. I was only letting you know that I knew."

"But how would you know if I don't?" I stood, pressed a shaking hand to my forehead.

"That's true. It appears you're still early." His gaze slipped to my mid-section.

Instinctively, I crossed my arms over my belly. "How do you know this? I mean, why do you think this?" I stammered.

There was always the possibility that Dr. Rivera was utterly shitting me for some reason. The power of suggestion, like many magicians used. A mental trick to get people to divulge information themselves. It hadn't occurred to me until now but maybe he was mentally ill himself.

All I knew was that I had the sudden urge to go find out. To leave this house and drive to the nearest CVS and buy a pregnancy kit. Was he psychic all this time and just fucking with me?

"The angel statue," he said, all of a sudden.

"What about it?"

"The lantern glows bright whenever a pregnant woman is near." He seemed proud of himself when he said this, like he was imparting Harding Estate trivia during a ghost tour. "You were standing next to it last night, remember? When Barbara and I went outside to meet you, you had just been touched by Julia, you said."

"Attacked is more like it."

"Okay, attacked. *Lo que sea*. Anyway, *ten cuidado* is all I'm saying. Be careful with Julia. If she knows you're pregnant, you may suffer."

I sat up straight and pushed my silverware from me in final gesture. "I don't need to be careful with her anymore, Dr. Rivera, because I'm done in this house. I'm going home. The only reason I'm sitting with you now is because I fainted and woke up starving, or else I would've left already. Don't take that personally, but I've done all I can. It's time for me to go."

And pee on a stick—STAT.

He nodded. "*Sí*, I understand. Do you prefer cash, or is a check okay?"

"Cash if you have it," I replied.

Was I really pregnant? A million thoughts swirled through my mind—of telling Samuel, of telling my parents, all my friends, of wanting to move to a new house, make a proper start for the baby. It would make sense after how I'd been feeling since yesterday—the

119

soreness, the boobs hurting, the nausea. It would also make sense that I'd connect with Julia Harding's spirit if she'd been pregnant after all.

Maybe the ghosts, like Dr. Rivera, had been trying to warn me. What did the pale blue dress lady say, among other things? *Especially in your condition?*

While Dr. Rivera left the room to go fetch my payment, I snuck into the ballroom, exited through the service door, and went outside for fresh air after a stifling thirty minutes in the dining room. I had to see the angel statue for myself, see if the doctor had been right and wasn't just a batty old dude pulling my leg.

Though it was getting dark, I strode into the garden and found the angel statue looking as melancholy as I had last seen it. Staring at the angel's face, I waited to see if the light would come on.

"Well?" I asked after a minute of nothing happening. Maybe I'd just been lied to. Maybe it had been the power of suggestion after all, to make me spill a truth. But why would he care if I was pregnant or not?

The nightly ocean air felt warm though cooler than yesterday, and my whole body chilled. I hugged myself in the breeze. "Julia, are you here? Am I really pregnant?"

I couldn't believe I was talking to a tombstone angel statue to find out what should've and could've easily been verified via Science at the nearest convenience store. This was absurd, and I had to go. But suddenly, something dropped from the roof and landed by my foot.

A pebble.

I picked it up. Just an ordinary tiny stone falling off the roof. Loose debris getting blown by the breeze. I glanced up anyway and nearly lost my breath when I spotted the silhouette of Mrs. Rivera staring out her bedroom window, as still as a statue herself, backlit by a soft glow.

In the darkened window of the room next to her, a curtain fluttered slightly, like an air conditioner or fan blowing the drapes, except it stopped after a moment. At this point, I had to question my exhaustion and fragile state of mind. Wasn't that what Bibi had said? That I could become vulnerable here?

Still, I couldn't remember where that room with the billowing curtain was in the house. My mind went over the upstairs floor plan and all the rooms I had cleaned while doing the *despojo*. I didn't remember seeing that room with the curtain nor could I even figure out how to access it from the upstairs hallway. This would require another look inside the house.

Turning back to the angel, I half-expected Julia to be standing there or see her hanging from a tree or any of the other horrible sights I'd seen today. But the garden stood empty, tall grasses swaying in the draft.

"Julia," I said. Somehow, I had to make peace with this spirit. If I really was pregnant, I hate to go home with a vengeful ghost following me. "I'm sorry for everything that happened to you. I'm sorry if you really were pregnant when you passed. But here's something that might make you feel better—I have a message. From Roger."

I waited. For a split second, I thought I noticed the angel blink at me.

"He says he's waiting for you on the other side. He wants you to leave this plane and go be with him, Julia. He loves you. We all do. You'll feel better if you go. You don't need to suffer anymore."

It occurred to me then, having grown up Catholic and hearing about the souls of those who'd committed

121

suicide, that maybe she couldn't move on. Maybe she was stuck here, condemned to all eternity because she'd taken her life. Banned from the Kingdom of Heaven.

"I don't think it's true, Julia," I said. "You're allowed on the other side. You can join Roger in the Light."

And then, it happened again.

The dim light of the angel's lantern grew brighter and brighter, too bright for such an old lamp, until I had to shield my eyes. A light this bright could probably be seen from sea. After a few moments, it died down.

Julia could hear me.

I wouldn't stick around to test if the lantern-pregnant theory was right by asking a bunch of questions. My visit was getting creepier by the second. As per my habit whenever I was nervous, I plucked at my lucky Buddhist bracelet on my wrist and realized it had gotten even tighter overnight. Water retention much?

I headed back to the house.

Dr. Rivera was waiting for me in the living room. "Are you sure you want to leave? My wife, she has a beautiful private collection of art she created to mourn the loss of our baby."

"I'm sure it's gorgeous, but I really do have to go. My husband will want me home soon."

"Oh? He's back from his trip?"

It unnerved me how much he knew what he shouldn't have known, but that was my own damn fault for talking too much.

"Yes, and he'll be very upset if I'm not home soon." I tried appealing to his machismo sensibilities—the little woman getting in trouble with her husband if she wasn't home soon. Surely, this was one item on which we could agree.

"Ah, *bueno*." He threw up his hands in defeat, as though he'd tried his best. I felt sorry for him. He might've just wanted company.

I went upstairs into the gaudy jewelry bedroom and collected my things, shoving them into my bags haphazardly—the bottles of herb blends, candles, hairbrushes, dirty shirt...

I could fix it all when I got home. The thought of going back to the apartment and sleeping there all alone made me equally as nervous as staying in this creepy house. Samuel wouldn't be home for another two days. At least here, I wasn't alone.

Rushing downstairs before any more ghosts could manifest for my attention, I found Dr. Rivera waiting for me in the living room. He cocked his head and held out his hand for a handshake.

"Miss Quey*lín*, it was a pleasure to meet you. I'm sorry you won't be seeing my wife's private collection. She doesn't show it to too many people and was hoping to get your reaction." I wondered how he knew what his wife wanted and was thinking when the poor woman couldn't even speak or move.

The brain is a powerful thing indeed, Dr. Rivera.

The doctor handed me cash. Considerably more than he'd offered. A thousand, to be exact.

"This is unexpected," I said.

"I've given you a hard time, *niña*."

Out of the corner of my eye, I saw Lovely lingering by a wall near the staircase. She wrung her hands, watching me interact with Dr. Rivera. I gave her a little smile as if to say it was nice meeting her, and thank you so much for introducing me to the dead man upstairs.

"Thank you." I held up the bills. "Are you sure this is the right amount?"

"Yes. I know I'm a cranky old man and you didn't deserve my interrogations or for me to *regañarte*."

To punish me or give me a hard time. No, I didn't deserve it, especially when I was doing him the favor.

"Especially when you were the only person out of seven who I went to who would come out," he added.

"I'm sorry?"

"I asked seven people. Psychics, ghost hunters...whatever you want to call them. They don't like coming out here. Surely you knew this house had a reputation."

"For being haunted, yes, I did. But lots of people love exploring haunted houses."

"Not this one. Not in the fifteen years I've lived here."

So the psychics who'd visited had all come before Dr. Rivera's occupancy?

Something in the doctor's smile chilled my skin and made me feel like I'd walked right into a trap. Like the last two days had been nothing but an illusion of me thinking I was free to move around when really I was a rat in a large cage. I shook it off. If that was true, he wouldn't be saying goodbye to me now, paying me for my time.

Walking to the front driveway felt liberating.

I threw my things into the car, slipped in, and pushed the key into the ignition. I should've been surprised when my car wouldn't start. *No, come on. Come on, you piece of crap.* I smacked the bottom of the steering wheel gently while Dr. Rivera watched from the doorway. Like all good Cuban folks, they waited while you drove away and only disappeared into the house once you drove out of sight.

Dr. Rivera lingered. Now I would have to suffer the humiliation of my car not starting while he looked on.

"Everything okay?" He stepped over to the car. "Want me to take a look? I used to be pretty good at fixing my own. Here, step out and I'll see."

I hated the thought of needing this man to get inside my personal space to solve my problem and wondered why I never took that basic "car trouble" course my college offered back when I took classes.

"Thanks, it's weird. I just bought this car." Granted, it was two years old, but still. Why did it have to fail tonight of all nights?

"Yes, but that's what cars and most technology does best. Test our patience." He slipped behind the wheel and tried starting it. Then, he popped the hood, scrambled out, and stood in front of my car, staring into it.

As he worked the problem, I hugged myself in the chilly night and wondered what to do in case my car wouldn't start. I'd have to call a Lyft to come get me or see if Bibi or Maggie could come pick me up. I couldn't tell my family, because that would require having to explain my crazy mission.

Standing there wishing this night would end, I caught a glimpse of something in the driveway. Shiny and embedded between the brick pavers. I walked over to it and squatted. A long piece of cut quartz without its chain.

Glancing at Dr. Rivera to make sure he was too busy to notice me, I picked it up and turned my back to him to examine the stone in the light. It was a familiar stone, Bibi's quartz, the one she always kept on a chain around her neck. I searched for the chain and found it near the spot where the quartz had been.

A piece of the chain anyway.

Why would there be a *half* a chain and not a whole one? If my necklace were to fall off, I'd think it'd break in one spot, causing the thing to slip off my neck. It wouldn't be broken into multiple pieces.

There'd been a struggle.

"*Hija*, I think it's your battery but it could also be your alternator. Do you want to wait inside while I go find some jumper cables?" Dr. Rivera took out a handkerchief from his *guayabera* pocket and wiped his hands and forehead.

My heartbeat kicked into high gear.

I didn't like finding Bibi's charm on the ground where she'd probably stood waiting for her ride, and I didn't like that she hadn't shown up at work, and a little while ago, a pebble had fallen from above, from a window. A curtain had moved from an unknown room.

I didn't like that either.

But I didn't want to clue the doctor in on the trepidation and fear I was feeling either, so I smiled, which might've been a dead giveaway considering I hadn't smiled all day.

"Sure, I'll wait inside."

"*Bien*. Give me a minute. I'll go find the cables."

I faked heading in, while he disappeared around the other end of the house between the south porch and a free-standing shed or separate garage.

The cables. Was he really going to go find the cables? Or something to hit me over the head with? I should leave, but if Bibi was here, I had to find her. I couldn't leave her alone. Shit—I had to stay.

And that upstairs room was my first priority.

When an old Cadillac drove up, and the doctor stepped out toting actual cables, my chest released a sigh of relief. He wasn't going to kill me. Not now anyway. I felt a surge of guilt that I'd thought of him in a negative light, but I couldn't be too careful. Not until I located Bibi.

The doctor opened his hood and connected the cables between his battery and mine and smiled at as if to say, see? I'm being cavalier and helping.

Maybe I was overreacting. It'd been a long two days, and if I really was pregnant, then the hormones plus exhaustion wasn't doing me any favors.

I glanced at the upstairs windows of the house. From here, I couldn't see the two rooms I'd watched from the garden. What if Bibi was up there right now, unable to speak, lips fused together, trying to get my attention? I texted her right there on my phone and waited for a reply.

Nothing came.

When the doctor couldn't get my car started, I wasn't at all surprised.

"You know," I said, carefully exploring all my options, of which there weren't many. "I think it'd be fine if I stayed another night. Your wife's art collection does seem like something I'd find interesting, after all, and tomorrow I could call someone to come get me. Would that be okay?"

My ulterior motive wasn't to sleep over again. Not in a million years. It was to buy time. Get upstairs. Wait until everyone was asleep, then search the house for Bibi. Leave unnoticed after that, regardless of whether or not I found her.

"Sure, no problem." Dr. Rivera smacked his hands together to shake off the dirt. "But won't your husband think it's strange? I mean, since he's back home from his trip and everything?"

The doctor smiled.

FIFTEEN

"He'll be fine with it." My fake smile belied my hesitation. "He's asleep with jet lag anyway." As if there was much jet lag between Chicago and Miami. My lie was completely see-through, I knew that, but I pretended to be absorbed by my phone screen, just so our eyes wouldn't meet.

"Jet lag, eh. Well, as long as you're both okay with it." Dr. Rivera shrugged, closing up the hoods of both cars and handing me back my keys. When his hand lingered in mine, I looked up at him. He stared amusedly into my eyes. "I'll have Lovely prepare your bed again."

"Great, thanks." I tried to ignore the feeling of dread creeping up my back, like I was about to enter a burning building without a smoke shield.

The old man ambled into the house first, while I waited a beat out on the driveway to see if I could find anything else of Bibi's. More signs of struggle, more fallen objects from her purse, anything.

"You coming?" he asked.

"Yep." I casually followed him like nothing was wrong, stepped into the house, my eyes roving the living room, the wall connected to the staircase. If God forbid, Dr. Rivera really had abducted Bibi, he probably wouldn't have taken her through the front door where I'd been performing the spiritual cleansing. He would've dragged her around the side, put her in that outside garage, maybe driven her somewhere else.

But I visually examined everything I could while making my way to the stairs. *Please, universe, let clues jump out at me, if there are any.* Seeing nothing special about the gorgeous interior of Dr. Rivera's old tropical home, I headed to the stairs. Once I felt it was safe and nobody's prying eyes were on me, I'd try and find the room I'd missed while cleaning, the one I'd seen from the garden.

I couldn't get over how surreal it was that I even had to do this. My life had shifted from white to gray in the course of one day. I headed upstairs, locked myself in the bathroom to catch my breath, and saw my own reflection.

I looked tired. Was that woman looking back at me really pregnant? I'd always wanted to be a mother. Samuel and I had talked about it many times, but I never wanted to find out from a creepy, old man who argued religion and the supernatural with me.

Sitting on the toilet lid in the privacy of the bathroom, I did the first thing that came to mind, and not what one would think while sitting on the toilet. I called Bibi. Her phone went to voicemail, which wasn't at all strange. She was twenty-one and preferred texts like everyone else of her generation, except she didn't answer them this time.

I took a photo of her quartz crystal and was about to send it to her, asking if she was missing it when it occurred to me not to give details away. She would *know* if she was missing it.

Hey, hon. I know you left in a hurry, but did you lose anything important? I texted.

And waited. No reply. In fact, my last text went from blue to green, indicating she'd either turned off her phone, or it'd gone dead.

Before unnecessarily alarming Bibi's family, I tried something else—I held the crystal in my hand and closed my eyes, clearing my mind of as much distraction as I could, given the situation. If I had even a fraction of Rain's talents, I might be able to see what happened to Bibi the moment she lost her necklace in my mind. But I wasn't that talented, and I must've tapped out any new abilities over the last two days, because I couldn't pick up a single thing.

All I could see was Bibi lying unconscious in a room, but I knew that was fear, not reality. My fears *always* hijacked my brain. Fear of not having enough money, fear of losing my husband, fear of alienating my family through my new beliefs.

Fear—always the freaking fear.

Outside the bathroom, feet shuffled inside the guest bedroom. I could see quiet shadows moving underneath the door. Lovely was probably preparing the bed for me. Even though it wasn't necessary, having another human nearby was comforting. I waited until the footsteps left my room before calling Samuel.

I needed to hear his voice at this moment more than anything. "There's my gorgeous girl. Been busy, huh? I've been sending you pics all day about the conference and nothing."

"Babe, the weirdest things have been going on." My voice sounded tired and shaky. If I were him, I'd be concerned about me right about now.

"What is it? Tell me." His voice shifted from jovial to worried.

"You know how I'm always wondering when or if I'll ever see a ghost like half the people I know?"

"You saw one," he guessed.

"I've seen like four, babe. *Four.* Not only that, but I was finally leaving this house tonight when I came across Bibi's charm lying in the driveway."

"The pendant she wears?"

"Yes, the one she *never* takes off. The one she'd go on a worldwide crystal-hunt for if she were ever to lose it. Why hasn't she come back for it, or called me to find it for her, or text to ask if I've seen it? This thing means everything to her."

"Maybe she hasn't noticed it's gone?"

"Babe."

"I don't know, Quey. Maybe she's too scared of that house to go back? Why, what do you think?"

Sucking in a deep breath, I glanced up at the ceiling and pinched the bridge of my nose. "I don't know. I might be overthinking this, but what if she never left the house?"

"What are you saying?"

"Sam, she hasn't returned my calls, only texted back once when she first left. Said she had a headache. That was before her phone died, but what if it wasn't her sending those texts? What if…ugh."

"Say it."

"What if someone has taken her phone?"

I couldn't believe I was actually suggesting this. It sounded absurd but entirely plausible all at once.

"Queylin, you need to leave that house now."

"I can't. I need to see if she's here."

"Leave the house and call the police. Do it, now."

"Babe, listen…"

I'd unnerved him—understandably. I couldn't make him come home from the most important convention of the year, one that might possibly advance his career, all because I was a little nervous.

"It's fine. I'm going to take a cursory look around the house once everyone's asleep. Hopefully, it's nothing, and this is a case of 'better-safe-than-sorry.' But if I see anything suspicious, I *promise* I'll call the cops and get the hell out of here."

"*Run* the hell out, Quey. Don't wait for anything, not even a cab. Shit, I knew I shouldn't have let you go alone. I had a bad feeling about it, and I didn't tell you."

"Yeah, you only told everyone at the store."

Pause. Silence.

"I only did that because I was concerned."

"Because you didn't trust me, you mean."

"Are you serious right now? So, you're seriously mad at me, because I worried for my wife?"

I couldn't get into a fight with him now of all times. But that was exactly why he'd contacted the employees at the store—because he'd thought I needed backup. He'd thought I couldn't handle it.

"Look, I'm telling you I'm fine. I just want peace of mind that Bibi's okay, not locked up in a room somewhere, hoping someone will find her. Trust me."

Unless that's too hard for you...

"I do trust you. Whatever you need, call me. I can step out of any presentation. I can get on the next plane home."

A knock came at the bathroom door. I stared at it.

"You heard me?" Sam asked.

I covered my mouth over the microphone. "Yes. I'll call you back in a few. Somebody's knocking on the bathroom."

"I'd rather stay on the line until you know who it is."

"Yes?" I called out. "Someone's in here."

No reply.

If it was Lovely, which it probably was, letting me know there was a fresh towel for me or a glass of water at my bedside, she wouldn't be able to talk. Having Sam on the phone helped calm me, as I made my way to the door and slowly popped it open.

Nobody there.

If it had, in fact, been Lovely, then she probably took off after I took too long to answer. Either that, or the guest bedroom ghost was back.

"I gotta go," I told Samuel. "I'll keep in touch."

"Babe?"

"Yeah?"

"Be careful. Use your instincts. They've worked for you in the past. You don't need superpowers. You're smart already. You know what to do."

I smiled. "Thank you."

"I love you."

"Love you more."

Hanging up, I sighed and waited in the bathroom for a minute. Then, I strode into the room, mentally preparing to see the ghosts I'd come to expect. They were a part of this space, I'd learned, so I should never at any point assume I was alone.

Taking out my charger, I plugged in my phone by the nightstand, so it wouldn't die like Bibi's had. So I could call the police in a matter of seconds if I had to.

I lay down on the bed and stared up at the ceiling, scared of seeing the woman hanging upside-down like a spider, but even she couldn't hurt me. That was the thing with these ghosts—they could freak you out, they could startle the hell out of you, but they couldn't really do anything to you except mess with your mind.

The ghosts were merely distractions. It was real, live people I should fear.

At 8:30 PM, it was still too early for the house's residents to be asleep. I didn't know where Dr. Rivera and his wife had gone, but Lovely was downstairs making noises. Opening and closing drawers, clinking silverware, and shuffling her feet around.

I passed the time by devising a plan and texting Samuel emojis and a question. *Hey, I forgot to ask you, do you remember the first day of my last period?*

Not really. Why?

Just curious.

I didn't want to bring up the possibility of being pregnant over the phone, but I couldn't remember the first day of my last cycle. I usually got my period on the first day of the New Moon, but the last couple of months, my period had been out of whack.

Pinching the quartz between my fingers, I stared at the crystal and thought about what I would do if I were to actually find Bibi trapped in a room. Obviously, I hoped she wouldn't be, but what if?

I closed my eyes and imagined a white light of love and peace surrounding the house, filling each room, and especially covering Mrs. Rivera and Lovely. Hell, I threw one around Dr. Rivera, too, just in case my instincts were operating on overdrive, and he was nothing but a quirky old man with nothing to hide.

Couldn't hurt to envision good energy.

But I couldn't shake the feeling that there wasn't. Too many strange things about this house didn't add up. Like, who was the rosy-cheeked young woman in the photo with Dr. Rivera? Was he really that much older than his wife? Not that it was impossible. Young women married older men all the time, but…she couldn't have been old enough to leave Cuba as part of the Pedro Pan Operation of the 1960s, if that were her.

I was lying there, nearly falling asleep, the downstairs noises finally quiet, overwhelmed with the hellacious day when I heard it. From far away, at first, like from a dream.

Then closer. In the house.

Wake up, Queylin.

My eyes popped open at the sound. First, a baby crying. Then—a bloodcurdling scream.

SIXTEEN

Stepping into stillness and darkness of the upstairs hall, I stood at the top of the stairs, assessing where the sound had come from. It could've been downstairs, or a bedroom, or the ether itself. The house was quiet now. I must've fallen asleep.

All the bedroom doors were closed. I narrowed my eyes to see if there was another I might have missed when performing the cleansing, but from where I stood, there wasn't.

Five bedrooms in total upstairs.

Maybe a room existed *behind* the master? A connected sitting room, or office, or other space accessible only through that bedroom perhaps?

I waited for another scream, met only with silence. Unsettling silence. What did they do at night that the house sounded heavily unoccupied of human noises? Regular non-kitchen sounds, like coughing, or the TV, or toilets flushing, or God forbid, actual conversation?

But there couldn't be, I reminded myself. Because Dr. Rivera lived practically by himself with two women who couldn't speak. If I lived in muteness like that every day, I couldn't imagine how alone I'd feel. After a while, I'd start talking to inanimate objects like Tom Hanks to the volleyball, Wilson, in *Castaway*.

From somewhere in the distance, I heard the crying again, the one I'd detected in the master bedroom when I'd seen Mrs. Rivera staring out the window earlier, when Lovely scared me away. God, that felt like an entire week ago instead of half a day.

But that was the thing about the Harding Estate— reality, dreams, and dread all blended together. It was hard to tell where one started or the other began.

The crying came again, deeper, as though coming from the entrails of the home. It drove me insane with need to find out. I had to locate where it was coming from, knowing fully well I might not ever find out. As Bibi said, I might just have to accept that. Some ghosts would never be ready to move on.

I descended the stairs slowly, my eyes adjusting to the darkness as I went. A few candles were lit, flickering on their sconces, wax drippings collecting in bulky tails. *I know I heard a scream. It wasn't a dream.*

Determined to be fully awake, I was pretty sure that had been an actual scream. Dr. Rivera only wanted me to think otherwise. He loved messing with my mind. He'd wanted me to think these hallucinations were creations of my own brain, entities of my own madness. There was no doubt that was a possibility, but I had to follow my instincts.

Samuel told me they were good instincts.

And I believed there was darkness hidden in these walls.

Another cry emerged from the stillness, this one of a woman and more of despair, of subdued hopelessness, than physical pain. A helpless sobbing. My every nerve burned like individual fuses ready to detonate. I followed the sounds through the hallway, the servants' kitchen, and paused.

I closed my eyes for better calibration. The ballroom—the crying seemed to be coming from that direction. I stepped out of the kitchen, through the dining room, glad I had forgotten to put on my sandals. This way, I could silently wade across the wooden floors like a ghost in my own right.

I stopped at a china cabinet aglow on the inside with a soft nightlight. For a moment, it almost seemed like the crying was coming from behind it. Checking the wall behind the cabinet, I saw an electrical outlet and some dust bunnies but nothing out of the ordinary.

The crying stopped.

"Hello?" I whispered.

And waited.

No reply.

I was getting used to this house of no replies, no verbal ones anyway, but the home itself spoke volumes. I threw my hands into the action, letting my fingers slide across the cabinet and along the smooth, waxed dining table. I was always a tactile child who loved to touch everything, even got into trouble for it multiple times for accidentally breaking things my mother had been working on.

For years, I learned to keep my hands behind my back as my mother had asked, to stay out of trouble. But maybe that had been a suppressed natural instinct. I needed to touch things to hear them. I moved into the ballroom and touched the walls there.

A slight vibration coursed through me.

Energy.

No music played, no people danced, no servers roamed around offering hors-d'oeuvres, yet I could almost see them. See the parties, the hosts and hostesses over the years, the feathers, the dresses and tuxes, the delighted guests. I could almost feel the envy, the passions, the secrets of every person in the room, and yet the room was nearly empty, except for those stacked chairs and round, naked tables leaning against a wall.

And an armoire across the room.

A great big armoire that probably contained silverware, party platters, and tablecloths in every color. Or it could've been completely empty. I stepped across the beautiful parquet floors, imagining dresses, a slow waltz, gentlemen bowing, women laughing, drinks spilling. All the while, my eyes were riveted on the armoire.

The armoire.

It was a gorgeous, old, secretive piece, ignored, but intricately carved—loved at one time. I wanted to touch it, feel what it had to say, see if I could validate these odd impressions once and for all. All my life I'd had lucid dreams, instincts, only to find I'd been wrong or simply imagining things.

Had I been right—had I been right, just a few times, I might've cultivated my psychic abilities earlier. But I'd always been wrong. Which led to envy, jealousy, resentment for those who had them. For people like my own staff. In many ways, I hated them—hated my own employees. Women who were friends.

Fear. Fear of the unknown was the source of all problems.

Yet my friends, my witches, my *coven*, if you will, had accepted me, even though they knew I wasn't one of them. Not 100%. Yet they were supportive of my learning, of this spiritual journey on which I'd embarked three years ago. I had to get at least one impression right—if only for them. I didn't want to disappoint them.

Touch the armoire, Queylin.

From the corner of my eye, I saw a shape. A humanoid figure. My vision snapped right to it. Best to directly confront the ghosts. But no one was there. I resumed my slow walk to the armoire and stopped right in front of it, staring at it. It was larger than it seemed from across the room, a heavy, vintage piece of carpentry.

Did you see him?

Did you really see him?

I turned slowly. Someone was talking to me, not with a real voice. I didn't hear the words in my mind either. More of a whisper from somewhere inside my soul. I felt like I was in a waking dream.

Who? I asked.

Roger.

Julia was here with me.

"Yes, I did," I spoke aloud, my own voice sounding odd and echo-y in the emptiness of the ballroom. "He said he'd wait for you. You should go to him."

Maybe I could fulfill my purpose here after all and help these spirits find their rightful place in the cosmos. I used to think that haunting a home was romantic, gothic, even glamorous. I used to think how, when I'd die, I'd haunt a beautiful house such as this myself, but now I knew better. This poor woman was a prisoner.

A prisoner of her own fear.

"He's waiting for you," I told her.

She contemplated it. I couldn't see her or hear her anymore, but somehow I knew, she was contemplating leaving this existence, this plane that had given her nothing but a century of solitude.

They are barren, she said.

"Who?" I asked the emptiness. "Who's barren?"

For a moment, I questioned my own sanity. Here I was standing inside an empty ballroom at the infamous Harding Estate of Miami, talking to the air around midnight, using words I rarely ever used, like "barren," and hearing voices and cries.

I didn't know how long I stood there, but it might've been an hour. I listened with more than my ears, trying to gauge what it all meant. Was she gone? She seemed gone. Maybe Julia had moved on after all.

But then, her voice returned.

All of them.

Because of me.

And then, the armoire doors yawned open by themselves. Slowly creaked open, exposing a gaping, dark interior, no shelves, a few things on the bottom covered in dust. My heart beat fervently in my own ears. I heard the swooshing of my own blood through icy veins, as the armoire called to me.

As in many of my dreams, I was paralyzed.

But why? I'd sought this room out, this armoire. I'd made a conscious, waking decision to come here, to solve a problem, to experience firsthand what I'd always imagined I could never. Coming here had been my choice, and now that a ghostly armoire had opened its doors to me all by itself, now I was going to freeze?

No.

This paralysis, this fear of *success*, would not control me. Yes, Dr. Rivera, the mind was a powerful thing, so powerful, in fact, that we could do whatever the hell we wanted in this life, but first we had to get past the enormous obstacle of our own damned selves.

I could do this.

I took slow steps toward the armoire. The cavernous interior was hard to see, but there were platters, serving dishes, a row of dusty champagne flutes, and a stack of cloth napkins. When I blinked, the napkins were stained—in red. Bright drops of red on ivory satin, spreading through the fibers. Inside a silver serving dish, something moved.

I got closer and held my breath.

Barren.

Who?

All of them.

Because of me.

Inside the tray, something moved. Something covered in dark red, something congealed in fleshy lining and blood, something with tiny limbs giving into their last impulses, pumping and gasping and trying to survive, wrapped in its own umbilical cord.

I drew a breath and covered my mouth, suppressing a scream. My stomach writhed in a tight knot, as I sucked in deep breaths of stagnant air, fighting down the warm saliva pooling in my mouth. But then, the pain, the anguish of having lost this child, of having built my dreams around him, all came crashing inside my chest, and I dropped to my knees.

But I'd never had a child.

I'd never built dreams.

These thoughts did not belong to me.

But these women had. All of them—the ones who'd lived in this house. I had to snap out of it. Julia and the ghosts of this house, and Dr. Rivera himself, were all messing with me. I was stronger than this. I couldn't let one vision bring me down.

Gripping the armoire, I hoisted myself up to standing and faced the silver tray again, the baby taking its last breaths. There was nothing there. Just folded napkins and platters and fondue forks and dust. Lots of dust over it all. This armoire contained the expired dreams of countless women.

And at the very back was the oddest thing I had ever seen. Connected to the back wall, sticking out like a spout of the same dark brown color as the wooden armoire was a knob with a handle turned vertically. I reached out and touched it.

Vibrant energy sizzled through my fingertips.

Yes.

Wrapping my fingers around it, I turned the knob, and when I did, I felt the whole of the large piece of furniture lunge, squeal under its own weight, and let out a massive sigh. Hissing on hinges I couldn't see, it moved toward me, swiveling outward, the house's own doorway into another world. Slowly, it swung out, hovering over the floor, and I hadn't noticed that its feet never actually touched the ground.

And then there was a tunnel.

Dimly lit and long, tall enough to walk through but one would have to crouch to navigate it. Interior walls were paved with brick, and the air whooshing out the tunnel felt cold, but it was the music, the music emanating from the bowels of the house, that drew me in.

Music from another time and era.

Un son cubano playing on a Victrola.

SEVENTEEN

Two choices presented themselves—turn back and pretend I never saw this, or walk through the tunnel. If I turned back the way I came, I would never find out who was crying or why, might discover on the news that Bibi had gone missing then regret abandoning her for the rest of my life.

I could also proceed but find myself trapped, same way she might've been. There really wasn't a choice. I could never desert someone who needed my help. Holding my breath, I proceeded carefully, slowly. If I saw something potentially dangerous, I could always turn back, try a different method of helping, run back to my room to call the police.

I would've called by now, but I didn't have evidence, and I couldn't exactly tell the officer I'd been having "gut feelings" all day. One broken necklace wasn't exactly evidence. Finding out what was at the end of the tunnel would at least let me know what action to take.

Lowering my head, I took slow steps and followed the sound of the music. The air grew cooler as I went, and the warm light at the opposite end grew brighter. Enough to light my path and keep me from feeling like I was entering a dungeon.

This tunnel or vent, or secret passageway, or whatever it was, looked like it'd been here a long time. Probably built with the house, possibly to hide the cellar from law enforcement during the rum-running days. It wasn't common for Florida homes to have basements or cellars. Our grounds consisted of water-logged limestone, but some old homes had them for that exact reason—bootlegging.

A soft breeze cooed through the tunnel. I stopped several times to listen. I didn't want to simply appear at the exit and find myself face-to-face with disaster. I prepared several excuses in my head just in case Dr. Rivera should discover me here.

I was sleepwalking.

I heard a noise.

Wanted to make sure everyone was okay.

The ghosts told me to find this room.

None of them sounded convincing enough, and I knew, if caught, I'd anger the man of the house.

A few feet from the end of the tunnel, which must've run about twenty feet at a slope, I stopped, inching forward, wishing I could send my eyeballs ahead of me to peer into the room first. When I reached the end, I listened. For human noises, throat-clearing, footsteps, anything, though it was hard to pick up subtle sounds over the music. I was scared of what I might find but pushed through the fear.

I reached a sort of metal sliding door, closed over the tunnel exit, but not locked and with cut-out holes to let in light. This allowed me to see into the room from behind the relative safety of an ajar door. The room was well-lit—an art studio, from the looks of it, which relaxed my fears considerably. Even through limited visibility, I could see dozens of paintings set to dry all over the room, a few more up on easels in various states of completion, art lamps, and dozens upon dozens of cubbies along the walls.

I waited a long time before moving, and it occurred to me that I'd left the bedroom a couple of hours ago. I must've been moving through the tunnel at the careful rate of five minutes per inch. I couldn't mess this up. If I was going to trespass in private rooms, I was going to do it right.

When I did finally move, it was to slowly slide the metal door to one side, wide enough to creep through. I pushed my head inside and checked the room from one side all the way to another. The room was U-shaped, the center part being what seemed to be a dark, defunct fireplace. Fireplaces were about as useful in Miami as basements and cellars, but the first millionaires to move here from Chicago and New York City didn't know that at first, so the historic homes all had them. Also, a hundred years ago, the average air temperatures here were way cooler.

In the corner of the room was the old record player with the fluted bugle, just like I'd pictured it in my mind. I couldn't imagine Dr. Rivera playing music like that off a digital device and was happy to see the real vintage deal. But I hadn't come for the Victrola; I'd come because I'd heard someone crying, but one glance around the room showed it was empty.

The lingering smell of cigar smoke told me that Dr. Rivera did use this room, however, and could be back at any given moment. I had to explore quickly. Another smell permeated the space, but this one was harder to pinpoint. Something chemical. A cleaning product of some kind. Could've been turpentine for the paints.

The paintings were all of naked women. Beautiful women. Young women but also mature ones. All in various states of undress. Some younger ones folded their arms over pregnant bellies, some lounged on chaises like Rose in *Titanic*. All of them were elegant and tasteful and looked like something that should've hung in a museum gallery.

Barbara Rivera was a talented woman, no doubt. It was sad to see her so disengaged. I was glad to know she at least had art to keep her going. But why were these works so hidden? Why not keep her studio out in the open where I'd imagine it'd be easier to wheel her in and out? He couldn't navigate the wheelchair through that tunnel. There had to be another entrance.

On the far wall was the current work in progress, a large painting about eight feet tall, four feet wide, big enough to hang on a great room wall of a mansion such as this one. A main showpiece. The woman on the canvas was stunning, with lanky arms and legs, long brown hair, and the face of a porcelain doll. I felt like I'd seen her before. A movie star from days past.

She stood with her knee up and resting on a bed's edge, a pose which covered her most womanly areas. The model was nude like the others, both arms cradling a pregnant belly, but the belly itself was not finished yet. Not the belly, nor the legs, nor the lower right quadrant of the work.

The subject's eyes gazed into mine, as if expressing how incredibly happy she was waiting for this child, and I wondered if creating scenes like this helped Barbara deal with her loss. As I crept closer, I realized it wasn't really a painting at all, more of a bas relief carving or something involving sheets of crepe paper layered over each other to create a sense of depth and texture. Whatever it was—it was exceptionally beautiful. On a table facing it were the layers themselves laid out for the next part of the process, and scattered all around were tools—scissors both large and small, a sharp poking tool, a blunt one like a hammer.

I heard a whooshing, like wind traveling through cracks in the walls, or through the cubbies themselves. Upon closer inspection, the cubbies were actually the deep slots used for wine bottles in a cellar. Well, well, well. So, this was the room that didn't exist? The one filled and sealed after Hurricane Andrew.

Sure, I could see that, Dr. Rivera.

What was so secretive about it? It was an amazing room, probably the most interesting of the house, and this collection was simply stunning, as he'd said it was. Maybe he'd felt bad about barking at me earlier which was why he'd offered to show it to me, but then he would've had to admit that he'd been lying about the cellar being closed.

Many of the wine cubbies contained what looked like rolled-up sheets of paper scrolls. I cautiously stepped over and pulled one out, unrolled it, and stared into a sad pair of eyes. One after another. More beautiful faces, these captured in charcoal. Each sketch of a gorgeous face was covered by a sheet of wax paper to protect from charcoal smudging. But each also had a paper clip attached to the top right corner. I turned the sketch around to see what the clip was holding—a cutting of natural hair.

One after another, the rolled-up sketches all held wisps of dark hair, blond hair, auburn hair, straight hair, shocks of curls clipped to the back. Did his wife really keep mementos of the hair of each model she drew? Why would she do that?

I shuddered and put the scrolls back, rubbing my arms in the chilly room. My goal wasn't to check out her weird art anyway, in the studio built into the room that supposedly didn't exist—it was to find Bibi. I searched each corner, looked inside the cubbies—for what, I wasn't sure. I even checked the fireplace, which reeked of remains of charred wood.

Something glittered from underneath one piece of wood. I reached in and pulled it out. A necklace—a basic thin gold chain with a cross hanging from it. I dropped it right where it was and stepped away, trying to come up with any number of reasons why something like that would be there in the fireplace. Next to the dark opening was a short stack of wood.

I almost didn't hear the sound that came next because of the music that was playing loudly, and by the time I saw the front end of the wheelchair and pair of legs being pushed into the room from behind the current painting, I ran back to the tunnel, climbed inside, and slid the door over me.

My heart pounded. I prayed that nobody had seen me. Through the small slits of the metal door, I watched as Dr. Rivera wheeled his wife in and placed her in front of her painting. He spoke to her in Spanish but so quietly and lovingly, it was hard to hear, especially with the Victrola playing near me. But he kissed the top of her head, turned to admire her work so far, and spoke to her at length about what she was creating.

Maybe now I'd finally hear her speak.

As I watched with my a ball in my throat, I realized what had been strange while glancing around the art studio at first. I hadn't seen any paint. Even now, glimpsing through my limited field of vision, I saw none of the usual paint tubes, bottles of turpentine, paint thinner, or trappings one might expect to find in an art studio. A canister contained paint brushes in various sizes, but aside from that, all that was being used for this piece of work were the layers of crepe paper.

But when Dr. Rivera lifted one up and held it up to the belly of the subject in the painting, I could see how thick it really was. Not crepe paper at all. In fact, the woman was made up of patches of flesh-colored bits of leather. I was having a hard time reconciling what that might be, when Dr. Rivera's hand stopped caressing his wife's hair.

He tilted his head at her, said something about her appearance, something quiet that my brain imagined might be, *Your hair is crooked today, amor.*

He proceeded to yank off her hair right off the top of her head. A wig. The old woman wore a wig, and he was fixing it for her. No wonder her hair had seemed too shiny to be real for a woman her age. No wonder she wore hats every time I saw her.

Dr. Rivera proceeded to put the wig on the table, lift one of his sharp tools, then begin scratching the top of Mrs. Rivera's skull with it, like one might scrape off stickiness, like extra adhesive or caulking. What the hell was he doing? And why did the back of this poor woman's head have the biggest scar I'd ever seen in my life?

EIGHTEEN

When you witness something you thought was true completely unravel and expose itself as a lie, you don't know how to react at first. What to think or feel.

No, was my first thought.

Denial. Denial that anyone would do something like this. That anyone would fake their wife. The more I watched the doctor fix the dummy's scalp, apply more glue to her head, then affix her hair back on, the more incredulous I felt. Also, the more attached to this hiding spot. Because the next thing you feel is fear that the same might happen to you, and right now, this hiding spot was my saving grace.

I could not let the old man find me here. From what I could tell, he'd created a doll. A doll, of all things, and told people it was his wife. How long had he lived this lie? Had he put her together just for me because I'd shown apprehension at coming here alone? Somehow, I doubted it. He treated her with such loving care, I had to think he'd had this wife replacement for quite some time.

Did this mean that Barbara Rivera never existed in the first place? Was she an imaginary wife he created? But, who then, was the woman in the photo with him?

Either way, I had to get out of here, use this opportunity that he was in the studio-cellar to run through the house looking for Bibi. How had he gotten in? Another door must've existed on the other side if he'd managed to wheel Barbara in here. This house was full of secrets, twists, and turns. I could stay here for weeks and not discover them all, I was willing to bet.

In horror, I watched Dr. Rivera kiss his creation on the cheek, pick up a paintbrush, pull open a drawer, and dab a palette of colors—eye shadow, blushes, and other types of makeup, like foundation and mascara—onto her face. I wished I could get a good look at her from my vantage point, to put two and two together and see for myself that it'd never been real to begin with, to prove to myself that it had always been an illusion, but her back still faced me.

He touched up Mrs. Rivera—or the doll of her—and stood back to assess his masterpiece.

Satisfied, he put the brush back in its container but then noticed something about her dress that he didn't like. He reached behind her, and, leaning her forward so her face mashed up against his stomach, unzipped the back of the dress. He pulled it off her slender arms with some degree of difficulty, and tossed it aside. The doll wore a bra from what I could tell, and I tried to get a good look at her skin. Where her spine was, I spotted a massive scar from base of neck to base of spine where it disappeared into a pair of underwear.

I couldn't see anymore.

Just that enormous scar running vertically along the back of her body like a wicked set of railroad tracks. A doll wouldn't have that. What the hell was she made of?

As she sat there nearly naked, I bristled at the thought of what he might do next. When I saw him

152

heading my way and whistling, I lay down under the exposed slots in the metal door and prayed to the Universe that he not discover me. I shook so hard, I thought he would hear me trembling inside the tunnel.

Please, God, Universe, please…

The music stopped, and I heard the puttering noises of someone taking a record off and flipping it over. After he changed the record, and a scratchy sound began, he opened a door that creaked and closed it again. His footsteps disappeared to the opposite end of the art studio.

I was safe for the moment.

The music that started this time was a piano concerto, something slow and melancholy. On shaky hands, I raised myself up, my whole body trembling, just so I could place one eye at the bottom corner of the metal door's slot. The doctor was back with Barbara, a freaking doll, dressing her in a new outfit—a black dress. This one also slipped on easily and zipped behind her back.

"We can't have the girl seeing you in the same dress again, can we?" I heard him say in Spanish this time, thanks to the quieter piano selection.

I knew I needed to exit the tunnel and seek what I'd come to find instead of watching this bizarre unfolding of events, but it was hard to tear my gaze away. I was riveted watching Dr. Rivera treat this figure with utmost care, talk to her, love her like she was real. Had he made it himself or ordered it from one of those creepy sex shops, because damn, some of those dolls really did look like the real deal.

But did they make old ladies?

I doubted it.

This one of Barbara, if such a woman ever existed, looked like a middle-aged woman who had aged significantly in a short amount of time. Like a person who had undergone a great amount of stress with lines around the eyes and mouth and all. No wonder he covered her face with hats. No wonder Lovely protected her at all costs, as she'd done earlier when I'd snuck into the master bedroom. She was the doll's bodyguard, to make sure I didn't uncover this weird truth. Or maybe Lovely had been hired to aid him in his delusion.

Did he think she was real?

Was the doctor really a patient himself?

Once Barbara was dressed and the old man seemed satisfied with her appearance, he turned toward the painting and considered it. Picking up one of his tools, he stepped up to the piece and dabbed areas coming off, used a different brush to apply what I guessed was adhesive, and pressed the lifted corner down.

Then, unfolding a stepstool, he stood on the first step and reached up to the subject's face. "She's got Elizabeth Taylor's eyes…" he sang, replacing the words about Bette Davis in a song from long ago.

He laughed to himself, applying a small piece of material to the canvas. Its eyes came to life with a purple hue, just like the famous Hollywood starlet with violet peepers.

It really was beautiful. But all this time, had Dr. Rivera been the artist, not his wife? Had he created *all* the paintings in the house or just this one?

He lifted a larger piece of material from the table and used the scissors to carefully snip off a smaller piece, all while humming to himself. Then, using his other hand, he reached for a bottle of clear liquid, poured some into a metal pan, then dipped the piece of material into it. The liquid had to either be an adhesive or cleaning solution.

Patting it dry on a blotched towel, the doctor resumed his position on the stepstool and added some more violet fabric or leather to the subject's other eye. Little by little, the woman's expression came to life with each added layer of this material. In one particular section of the painting, he tried bringing depth to the woman's hand by creating shadows underneath her fingers. Having a hard time creating the effect he wanted, he went back to the table and fished around a metal bin for a piece that would suit his needs.

When he lifted the bin and carried it to a sink to rinse off the pieces, my eyebrows drew a knot, as I watched the water drain from the edge. Red-tinted water that thickened the more he poured. He rinsed the pieces again and fished around for the right piece. When he picked one up, and I saw the way it flapped around, caught the back of it, the deep redness of the underside, my stomach took a dive.

I threw up onto the tunnel floor.

The material was skin.

In retrospect, I should've seen it was skin, but I never imagined it. Never thought it would be possible for a man I'd been speaking to for two days to be capable of using human skin in art. I didn't know for a fact that it was human skin, but it had to be. The pieces patched together to create the impression of human skin in the painting, so what else would it be?

But the eyes.

If he was using skin, then certain parts of the image, such as the eyes, had to be something else. Unless he painted the skin in the various hues that irises came in. But no, that looked like purple skin, and it all came at me at once, rendering the tunnel too warm to almost breathe in, as my stomach heaved again.

That was Bibi's skin.

Port wine stained skin was dark pink or purplish in color.

Jesus Christ, I had to get out of here. Just then, a door slammed and a bucket flew across the room, hitting the wine bottle cubbies and knocking to the ground. The doctor exclaimed in surprise then covered his head, as another item flew across the room. This time, a few of his metal tools.

Carving tools.

Tools he used on people.

Women.

Bibi.

Where was she? Where was my friend in this house of horrors? Had he killed her, and if he had, had he done it mercifully at least? Or had he simply removed the port wine stain and she was still here, alive somewhere in the house?

The cries.

Another item flew across the room by disembodied hands, and the doctor yelled at whoever was causing it. For a flash, I caught sight of the pale dress lady standing in the corner, angry fists balled, stringy hair hanging over her face. I wanted to join her in throwing things across the art studio. Part of me wanted to bust in and scream, show the doctor that I knew his secret, that he hadn't counted on one thing—my psychic sight.

That's right—*my* psychic sight.

I'd found this room purely because of it. I'd never have thought to look inside the armoire and locate a hidden latch that undid the back of the *mueble* without them. Never would've found this hidden tunnel or this awful room. But was it too late?

Now that I'd figured out the truth behind Dr. Rivera's strangeness, it'd mean nothing if I couldn't find Bibi. Alive or dead, I had to locate her. Just to know.

Spirits, where is she? I thought. *Where is my friend, the one who was here with me this morning? Please tell me.*

If they could talk to me about other things, perhaps they could tell me where Bibi's body was hiding. The ghost responsible for the poltergeist activity, the one right now plucking all the charcoal sketch scrolls out of the cubbies and making them fly for seconds before landing on the ground, stopped and stared at me.

As the doctor yelled at the ghost to leave him alone, muttered curses in Spanish at me for not being able to get rid of the nuisance spirits he'd hired me to rid, the pale blue dress lady zeroed in on me.

No, don't, I tried telling her. *Don't give me away.*

But before I could back up in the tunnel or scramble away, she lifted into the ceiling like a Palmetto bug in the corner of the room, drew in for momentum, then flew straight at me. Through the sliding metal door, she flew with her force, hurrying past me in a rush of frigid air that made me flinch inside the tunnel and gasp out loud.

She is in the house, the ghost said

Then disappeared.

Slowly, I turned my eyes to see if the doctor had heard me. And there he stood in the middle of the studio, tool in hand, cigar hanging from his lips, staring at me through the metal door slits with angry impatience.

NINETEEN

"*No te me vayas!*" he screamed, running at the door that provided me with minimal protection. "Don't you leave."

I scrambled the way I'd come, head ducked low, quickly through the passageway despite the awkward posture.

"Quey*lín!*" he shouted.

The way he insisted on saying my name this way said it all. He did things however he damn well pleased, just like he'd insisted on drilling Bibi about her port wine stain. No respect.

My terror magnified, my breath charged and echoed through the tunnel, my gasps loud in my own ears. He was behind me, keeping up, running with his head low. I looked back so many times, I didn't realize when I arrived at the end of the tunnel and found the armoire flush up against the wall.

I punched at it.

Stuck.

The old man was almost at me, and I was ready to turn around and kick him if I had to.

"Why are you running?" he asked, changing his screaming tone. "I'm not mad at you, Quey*lin*. Come here. Let me show you the collection."

Yeah, sure.

"I don't want to see anything of yours." I punched against the armoire that wouldn't budge and furiously scanned the walls for another way out, but I'd reached the end of the line.

I just want out of here.

"But you came in the wrong way. This door is one-way. You have to come out the other side. Come."

He slowed a few feet from where I stood, and for a second, I thought he was actually being nice, and I'd been running for no reason. Then I saw the scalpel or X-ACTO knife in his right hand and remembered he was a crazy mother-effer who used skin to create paintings.

I had to get out of here.

At that moment, I spotted the dangling end of a cord slithering up the wall, held in place with brackets across the ceiling. I yanked on it, and the armoire unlatched with a hiss. With everything in me, I shoved against it to get it to move until it finally swung open with its own weight.

Dr. Rivera reached me and grabbed my sleeve, pulling my arm toward him, but I twisted out of his grasp and stepped out of the tunnel, booking it across the ballroom. He might've been older but he wasn't slow and walked after me using long, aggressive strides that scared me more than if he'd jogged.

I'd reached the dining room by then, opening random drawers in the china cabinets as I went, hoping to find a useful knife.

The doctor appeared in the doorway from the ballroom to the dining room. "I don't understand why you are running. I'm not going to hurt you."

"You mean like you didn't hurt any of those women?"

"Which women?"

Playing dumb.

Buying time.

"The ones in the sketches. With their hair clipped to the back?" I backed out of the dining room, opening the last drawer on the way out and finding a cake server. As stupid as I'd look holding a cake server, it was pointy with a serrated edge and that was better than nothing.

He chuckled low and menacing. "You mean my patients? Barbara used to love sketching them back when she could still draw. She only kept their hair as an example for when it came time to paint. So she could get the hair color just right."

In a charcoal sketch?

I wasn't buying it.

"Your wife?" I asked incredulously. "You mean that *thing* in the cellar that's not a living human? Is she a doll you made?"

Slowly, I backed through the service hallway, between the dining room and kitchen. I had to keep my eye on him, keep up the conversation to buy time while I found a way out. Once the space opened up, and I found myself in the middle of the service kitchen, I spotted Lovely in my peripheral vision. She clung to the cabinets, one hand clutching her chest when she saw the doctor and I engaged in a cat-and-mouse game.

"That is my wife, Barbara, as you already know, Quey*lín*. She cannot fend for herself, so I have to do everything for her. Bathe her, dress her..."

I shook my head. "Are you serious?"

"You don't believe me?"

Did he actually believe Barbara was real?

I couldn't tell what was worse—that he was lying or that he believed his own lie.

There was no way that woman in the cellar was a real human being, yet he insisted on lying to my face. All the more reason not to believe a word he spoke. I had to go without finding Bibi, unfortunately. I regretted having to leave her behind, but it was time to save myself.

"Come. I'll show you," Dr. Rivera insisted. "She is incapacitated and depends on me and Lovely for everything."

Yeah, because she's not real, she can't move, and she has a giant track of staples going up her back.

The moment I made it safely out of the kitchen, I emerged in the living room and made my move. I bolted for the front door, praying it'd be unlocked. I'd be leaving my things behind, including my phone upstairs, but none of that mattered at this point. All I could hear was Samuel in my mind telling me he told me so, asking if I was *sure* I was alright. Because he could come home if I needed him to. He could call the police for me.

No, and no, and no.

I'd turned him down on every point.

My hardheadedness had gotten me here.

When I slammed into the door, the doctor turned the corner, coming quickly out of the kitchen, and sliding toward me with such resolute steps, I fumbled with the lock. It wouldn't open. I heard a series of electronic beeps and a whine and knew he or Lovely was controlling the door through an alarm panel, which made sense, because I turned my vision at that moment to see him touching the wall.

The door was locked.

He was coming right at me.

I stepped backwards over a low potted plant, nearly tripping, then again as my sandal caught on the corner of an area rug. Keeping my eyes on the doctor who wore a peculiar expression, one of amusement and pure annoyance, I navigated through the living room back toward the kitchen in this circle dance that seemed to never end.

Where would I go from here?

I tried my hand at the French doors—locked. I could run back the way I came, make it to the armoire and run into the cellar to find the "other" exit he'd mention, but this man knew his house better than anybody. Chances are he would appear in the cellar faster than I could.

The upstairs. I could escape through a window. I seriously doubted an eighty-year-old man would follow me, and even if he did, assuming we both fell, I'd have a better chance of surviving broken bones than he would.

"I don't know why you are you doing this, Quey*lín*. Let's discuss it. You're frightened, but I can explain. I told you there was no cellar, because my wife is very private about her art studio. She's—"

"There is no wife, Dr. Rivera!" I yelled, inching for the stairs. "What I saw in there was a doll, something you made, or…"

A corpse.

Why the idea hadn't occurred to me before, I wasn't sure, but I was certain it had something to do with positivity, my annoying proclivity to thinking the best of a situation, giving the benefit of the doubt. The same trait that had made me a good person in the real world made me a naïve fool inside the Harding Estate.

I didn't want to say it out loud, because that would only give him the chance to confirm or debate it, and I didn't want to discover that I was stuck in a house with a corpse wife glued to a wheelchair.

What would that mean for me?

I ran upstairs, saw the nameless ghost blocking the door to my guest bedroom, so I hooked a left into the master bedroom, locking the door behind me. Catching my breath, I pressed my ear to the door and heard the doctor giving Lovely orders to lock all exits and windows and make sure something I couldn't hear was guarded.

My hands and body shook so hard, I worried I might not be able to go on. This couldn't have been happening. And God no, I couldn't faint again, so I focused on my breath like I did in yoga class. Deep breaths, just this moment, nothing else. Deep breaths would deliver much-needed oxygen to my muscles and keep my heart rate even. Deep breaths would keep me focused on what I had to do.

Nothing else.

As doors slammed and more electronic beeps checked the status of exits around the house, I backed up slowly, the backs of my legs touching the bed. I turned and saw the window where I'd seen "Mrs. Rivera" sitting, "watching" the outside world. How could he insist his wife was real unless he was truly a sick man? A sick individual, living by himself in this corner of the world with nobody but a terrified, mute housekeeper to look after him. No wonder nobody had been able to learn much about the new owners in years.

Hearing his footsteps slowly coming up the padded stairs, I reached for a large dresser and slid it along the wooden floor it until it blocked the door. Then I ran to the back of the room and prayed there was some other way out. There had to be a back room. I'd seen from the outside. At first glance, there was no way of getting past the master bath area, but searching the doctor's closet full of nothing but men's suits, men's shoes, men's *guayabera* shirts, a door hidden behind the racks presented itself to me.

"Quey*lín*! Quey*lín*, open this door!"

Parting the suits, I checked for a handle. No handle but there was a latch. Removing the latch, I pushed open a stuck door and moved stealthily into a musty room, locked it behind me, and turned on the light switch, as the doctor continued to yell that he wasn't going to hurt me.

I looked around. It was either a private office or a storage room for keeping boxes and files.

"Bibi?" I whispered. "Bibi, you here?"

This was where I'd seen movement in the window when I'd been down in the garden, but there didn't seem to be anyone here. Furthermore, the windows were locked, bolted shut. I checked the only closet, found it to be full of cardboard boxes. There were many of them piled on top of each other, file crates on the floor, also sitting on top of a big wooden desk.

A cockroach, startled by the sudden company, skittered out of a box. I moved the cardboard lid off one of them and spotted lots of old files.

Pulling one out, I read:

Jazmin Echevarría, 2000.
Lillian Inez, 1999.
Hope Weatherford, 1999.

I put the lid back and reached for another box. These files were even older, from 1995 and earlier. With each box I opened, the more I went back in time, the more bugs would crawl out. Each file had a red tab in the corner. When I flipped open one file to see what the red tab indicated, on the back was a typed label—*no local family.*

Apparently, these had all been patients of Dr. Rivera at some point, before he retired, I guessed, and behind his desk, sitting by itself in a metal file sorter was a purple file folder. Pulling it out, I read Barbara Boudine, a file from 1976. She also had the red tab indicating no local family members, and when I opened the file, I recognized the woman's photo.

Barely recognized, but the resemblance was there. The doll? The framed living room photo?

In this pic, she was smiling and beautiful and fresh and alive, like in the "painting" he'd been working on in the cellar. It was the same woman as in the framed photo downstairs. I could see that now, the one I'd thought maybe was his daughter.

But I knew her from somewhere else.

The file contained all sorts of private information, including the type of medication he'd prescribed, all the symptoms of trauma disorder she'd experienced, and lots of envelopes. Greeting card envelopes. I opened one up, saw two little blue birds of an old greeting card proclaiming his love for her—neat handwriting in blue pen. Letter after letter of hearts and love and affection for this one woman.

Dr. Rivera was in love with his patient.

"But did he marry you, or take you prisoner?" I asked the photo. I brushed her face with my fingertip, feeling sad all of a sudden for whoever she was, as I got the sense that things had not ended well between them.

Both.

I looked up.

Who'd said that? Someone had spoken just now. One of the files sitting on the top fluttered in a breeze, even though the window was locked.

Another file moved, then another, softly lifting then settling down again, as though a rogue gust were moving them.

"Who's here?" I swallowed my fear. I had to face and speak to them. They weren't the ones who could hurt me, and it was about damn time I got over that.

He cared for me.

A woman spoke so softly, I almost couldn't hear her. She was reticent to speak, as if making any noise would cause her to give herself away.

I closed my eyes and did as I always tried to do when meditating—push away all thoughts, negative distraction, and live in the moment. *Just this.* I rolled my eyes up to the space between my brows and hoped that my Anja chakra would kick in.

"Speak to me," I said.

I waited, all the while aware that doctor's footsteps were pacing the hallways with greater urgency, doors opened and closed, and the old man was losing his patience looking for me.

I loved him, because he cared for me.

I had no one.

So I married him.

A woman appeared in front of me, filling the room with a cold so profound, I felt it in my bones. Felt my internal organs shrinking in an effort to stay warm. The windows froze over. Her features were familiar, a face I'd seen all over this house in different ways. Her eyes blazed with a violet inner light.

"I know you," I said. "You're from the bedroom. You came to me and Bibi last night." The young, beautiful woman with the luminous eyes. She was the one who watched me silently, who'd come to me with jewelry in her hands. The one in the "painting" made with skin.

166

Yes, she said.

"Was that yours? All that jewelry?"

Mine and every woman he's kept.

He keeps their personal items.

Kept? My skin prickled with anxiety.

"Did you really lose a child?" I asked. "He said you were pregnant." I wanted to make sure it was true, that he hadn't killed her instead. Part of me wanted to believe that it couldn't be all bad.

I did. I died giving birth.

And you will, too, if you don't get out.

TWENTY

My hands instinctively touched my midsection, shaking fingers splayed across my belly. I stared at her, trying to make sense of her words. How did she know? How could the ghosts know I was pregnant?

I had no time to ask her about it.

As the doorknob and door to the master bedroom shook with Dr. Rivera's rage, I had only a short time to figure out where to go from here. With the windows locked and no other rooms to enter, from what I could tell, it was a matter of time before he reached me. If not through the hallway door, then somewhere else, as this man must've had secret passageways to every part of the house.

The ghost cowered in the corner, squatting like she did in the guest bedroom. *He's coming*, she said. Did she not realize she was dead and could go anywhere she wanted?

"You don't have to stay here," I told her. "He can't hurt you."

He hurts everyone.

Shivers pricked up my spine. The man outside the master bedroom door really did intend to hurt me. I couldn't believe a word he said. So this had been his wife at some point, not just because he thought her to be. First she'd been his patient, then she'd married him, then she'd passed away while having his baby.

Not his baby.

He took me in.

"You're Barbara?"

Yes.

So Barbara Boudine had gotten pregnant, and the good doctor, in love with her, feeling the need to care for her, had married her out of goodwill. Her child had not been his.

The door rattled again.

Ven conmigo, she said in Spanish, urging me to follow her. She floated straight through the wall into the master closet. I hesitated going back the way I came, but being trapped inside a corner office wasn't helpful either. There was nowhere to hide.

Following a spirit into a closet, your mind starts to doubt itself, and everything about this house made me question my sanity. I was being led by Mrs. Rivera herself—the guest bedroom ghost had been my hostess all along. So who was that woman in the cellar? Was it really a doll?

No.

"No?" I questioned, even though I hadn't spoken aloud. Our minds were as one, same with Julia. I connected. I connected with spirits the way I always wanted to.

I cannot leave, she said.

"Yes, you can, Barbara. You're free!"

Not as long as he keeps me alive.

I understood.

He was keeping her "alive," wheeling her corpse around in a wheelchair, touching up her makeup, pretending she still existed. Barbara had been the patient? Seemed to me that Dr. Rivera needed a mental evaluation more than she did. Anybody capable of embalming a corpse to keep it around as a souvenir, all because he refused to accept the death of a loved one, was apt to do anything to keep his illusions going.

"The painting," I said.

With the flesh of others, she said, *he is bringing me back to life. You must jump through.*

Suddenly, a square door in the floor of the master closet flew open on hinges, and the ghost jumped into it, feet first, again as though she refused to believe she was dead. As if she possessed a flesh-and-bone body. If only I possessed a fraction of her same ability to float through walls and hang from the ceiling like a spider, I would've left a long time ago.

But ghosts didn't always know when they're dead, and Barbara was earthbound for a reason. A good reason. Someone would have to give her a proper burial and dispose of that flesh painting in order for her to be free, but not before handing it over to authorities for DNA testing.

A lot of women had suffered to bring that painting to life, no pun intended, and I was sad to think that Bibi may have been one of them. Looking down the open hole in the closet, it seemed like a narrow laundry chute. I wasn't sure I would fit the entire way down, but I also didn't have any other alternative.

I jumped.

And fell feet first into a dark room about ten feet below the ceiling, landing on my side. I would be bruised and battered if I survived this, but at least I'd be alive. The question was, would I make it out of here? There were only so many secret rooms a house could have, but I supposed it was better to be trapped inside the Harding Estate, where at least there were a million places to hide.

With the ghost of Barbara Boudine-Rivera apparently gone, I lay in darkness a minute, refusing to make noise or give away my hiding place. After all, the chute door above was still open, and the master of the house could peer down at me any moment. I should've closed it behind me, as I jumped.

I decided to crawl to the corner, so that if he did aim a flashlight or any light source into this room where I'd fallen, I'd at least be out of immediate sight. In a corner, I could cower while figuring out what to do next. Luckily, Dr. Rivera seemed to have left the master doorway. Maybe the dresser blockade had worked after all.

The moment I began navigating the dark, it was clear I wasn't alone. I couldn't see them, but I could feel them. I could also smell them, as I stumbled over limbs, legs, arms, and torsos, all of them cold and stiff. I covered my nose with my hand. No way. No damn way had I jumped headfirst into a room full of...

God, Universe, please.

I couldn't believe I was trapped in a room with the mother lode. Part of me still wished I would wake up from this dream, this nightmare, more like it, soaked in sweat, but at least it would not be real. I could laugh it off as that crazy hallucination I once had.

Not a chance—it was real, and those were legs that I'd tripped over. I reached around me for things to hold onto, my fingers gripping metal shelving units, water heater tubes, and other utility room things.

There was crying again—whimpering more like it.

It may or may not have been the exact same crying I'd heard earlier, but nonetheless, someone was alive in this room with me. One person, at least, possibly more. The faces of all the charcoal sketches haunted me in the darkness. I could see them all staring at me, begging me to help them, or crying because I hadn't.

"Who's in here?" I whispered.

My hand felt the wall for a light switch. If I could turn one on for only a moment, I might see where the door was, maybe be able to get out—get us all out—whoever was in here with me, whoever was crying in the stifling heat and darkness.

The sniffling continued. Whoever was here, she was too weak for words. But at least she was alive, assuming that was real crying, not ghostly tears. I fumbled in the dark, felt my foot touch a body that seemed warm and pliable compared to the others and reached down with shaking fingertips.

"Who's this?"

A woman moaned. She didn't seem to be aware of her surroundings. The slippery bottom of my sandal slipped on a slick surface, and I gripped a shelf to keep from falling. Metal items and aerosol cans rolled to the floor. My hand felt out the shape of a doorknob. I turned it, found it locked, and instinctively turned the lock. The door opened without any effort.

I kept it open slightly to let in just enough light to see without alerting anyone to the fact that I was in here—that *we* were in here. And then I saw her, writhing on the floor, moving her hands slowly, trying to wake up. Short, blond cropped hair, blue fingernails…

"Bibi!" I whisper-shouted.

Weak eyelids looked up then, narrowing as they adjusted to the fresh rays of light, and I saw her face— half of it had been removed. Half her skin was gone. Completely gone. And her face was red, raw, oozing with blood, bone showed through, but she was alive and shook her head softly from side to side.

I slipped in beside her.

"Bibi, you're okay, you're okay," I told her. Even though she wasn't, I wanted her to believe that she was, so she could get up, get out of this house, and run. "Did he hurt you besides here?" I touched a spot on her forehead still intact. "Shit, Bibi...shit."

Damn it, this had happened to her because of me, because I'd dragged her into this. I was so freakin pissed at myself, but this wasn't the time. This moment wasn't about me, and if I really felt all that remorseful then I would get her out of here and stay to deal with the doctor myself if it came to that.

But I had a general idea of where I was, had explored the house enough during the house cleansing to believe that the kitchen was to my right, and if we went out those doors, I might be able to unlock the back patio French doors, and run outside to the garden.

From there, we could find our way out.

"Queylin."

"Bibi, I'm going to get you out of here, okay? You have to walk, though. Can you stand?"

She winced in pain. "They're dead. They're all dead. What do we do?" She looked over her shoulder before squeezing her eyes shut.

I could see what she referred to, but holy shit, there was nothing we could do for those women. I squeezed out tears that rose and burned my lids. I gave them good thoughts. I prayed for their souls. But I could do nothing for them. I doubted any of them were alive anyway, but just in case, I used what little light filtered in to go around, one by one, touching each body to see if any were alive. I must've counted five bodies in the closet, but only Bibi felt warm. Only Bibi responded.

"They're dead, Bibi. We can't... I'm going to walk out and check who's out there. When you see me nod, you follow me out. We're going to get out of here." Grabbing her by the shoulders, I looked into her eyes. "You hear me? We're going...to get....out. Ready?"

She nodded.

God, she looked terrible. She'd be scarred for the rest of her life, in more ways than one. "I'm so sorry for this. But I'm so glad I found you." I threw my arms around her and cried into her shoulder, pulling back, forcing myself to stop. This wasn't the time for tears, and yet I was overcome with raw emotion.

"Wait for my signal."

Slowly, I stepped into the kitchen, my back against the wall. I tiptoed quietly into the room, squatting along the lower cabinets so as to avoid detection from the other side of the counters. All we had to do was make it to the French doors. Alarm or not, we could run outside into the coastal wilderness. Let the alarms sound. Let the police come. We'd be free.

We'd never be the same again.

But we'd be free of this horror.

I was halfway into the kitchen, almost to the other side, when the light snapped on. I stopped cold, blood draining from my face, and looked up. Lovely was there, waiting.

TWENTY-ONE

Our eyes met.

All this time, I hadn't been able to figure Lovely out. Was she frightened? Was she captive? Was she Dr. Rivera's loyal servant...what? She watched me carefully, and I saw the wheels turning in her head, wondering if she should report my presence to her employer? Doctor? Master?

As someone's footsteps headed up the living room near the kitchen, I shook my head. *No, please don't tell him.* Dark eyes flickered from me to her peripheral vision where I could hear Dr. Rivera heaving for breath.

"Have you seen her?" he asked, his voice deeper than usual.

Lovely stared at him, her hands clenched into a fist just under her breasts.

"Tell me, have you seen her!" he shouted. I felt his anger mounting and worried for the woman. For God's sake, Lovely, tell him yes or no, but answer him if you can. He wouldn't demand she answer if she couldn't speak, would he? At this point, I put nothing past him.

If he would've stepped into the kitchen right this moment, he would've seen me crouched next to the end cabinet, hiding in plain sight.

"Lovely?"

She wouldn't reply.

He stepped closer to her, reached into the kitchen where the butcher block stood on the counter and slipped out a large kitchen knife, pointing it at Lovely's chin. "I will only ask you once again, dear lady. Have you seen…the girl…in the house? *Eske ou te we ti fi a?*"

If Lovely's eyes widened any more, they'd have pushed out of her skull. Her whole body trembled. Couldn't he see that she was incapable of replying with even so much as a nod? The woman was so terrified, it was hard to watch.

Finally, the doctor gripped her face with his free hand, pushing her cheeks against her face bones, and pressed the knife into the corner of her mouth. With a swipe, he slid the point of the blade across the seal of her lips with a swift movement that had me wincing and looking away.

"Have…you…seen…her?" he asked through gritted teeth. "SPEAK!"

But Lovely couldn't. Even as her mouth gaped open, and she gasped for air. Her voice had escaped her, or she'd forgotten how to vocalize, or she was simply too scared of him. The doctor grabbed her by the hair and shoved her aside, slamming her against the French door.

Lovely's chest heaved, as a thin line of blood dripped from her mouth. Like a fish out of water, she gasped for huge breaths. Had he really glued her mouth shut?

"Useless," Dr. Rivera muttered and peered out the window, scanning the grounds. "I'll be back. Watch this door." He pressed a button on a small panel by the exit, disarming the alarm, and stepped outside.

Lovely looked at me again. It was hard to look back at her. He'd hurt her because of me. She'd taken a beating because of me. I didn't know how to thank her or what to say. I looked at Bibi lingering just inside the laundry room doorway.

"I'm going to move now. Wait for me," I whispered.

I crawled to the kitchen entrance closer to Lovely and peered outside. The doctor stood on the back porch smoking his cigar, knife dangling in his left hand, a smear of blood along the edge. Losing my nerve, I was about to go back the way I came. It was too close for comfort, as he could've re-entered the house at any moment.

But Lovely let go of the wall she was holding, took a few steps backwards, keeping her eyes on me the whole time, and bumped into an adjoining kitchen door. Opening it, she stood off to one side to show me it was a pantry. On its opposite wall was another door leading to the outside, complete with old jalousie glass windows.

If I thought about it too long, I'd lose my chance. "Let's go," I told Bibi, darting for the pantry, scampering across the short expanse of floor behind Dr. Rivera's field of view. We whisked past Lovely into the pantry, and if I'd had a moment to spare, I would've hugged her for this act of pure bravery.

But a second later, she'd closed the door gently behind us, and now we huddled together inside the closet just barely big enough for two people. I threw my arms around Bibi and couldn't help it—lost my shit and cried into her shoulder. I had to contain my stress, though, or the old man would surely hear us outside the door.

Straightening up, I looked Bibi in the eye and mouthed as quietly as I could, "The moment he comes back in, I open this door. You run out. You find the side gate. If it's locked, you run into the woods. Do not stop for anything until you've reached a person who can help you. Understand?"

She nodded but I could see that she was only half with it. Heavy eyelids told me she was coming out of being drugged, and the pain wasn't making its way back again. The left side of her face looked abysmal. Tons of surgeries would be required to help her look normal again, but I couldn't think about it right now.

I would never live this down, though.

Slowly, gingerly, I turned the lock on the knob, looking out the dirty jalousie windows. There stood Dr. Rivera spitting tobacco flakes from his tongue before turning and pulling on the French door again. This was it, our chance for escape. With a deep breath, I yanked on the door knob to set her free, but it wouldn't open, and that's when I saw a slide latch on the top part of the door that hadn't been unlocked.

Shit.

I reached up and undid it, but the sound had already alerted Dr. Rivera. Through the pantry door, I heard him asking Lovely what the noise had been.

The door was stuck with years of layered, thick paint, but I wrenched it free and stepped aside to let Bibi out. "GO!"

"Come with me," she said before darting out like a doe released into the wild, thin arms and legs pumping like mad, just as the pantry door opened, slamming me in the shoulder.

I cried out, scowled, and tried slipping out the door but the doctor's arm had reached around the door and grabbed my upper bicep. "There you are. Come here." His grip squeezed my arm.

I bit into his hand.

He let go.

Pulling the door towards me for momentum, I slammed it against his arm, and he cursed in seven languages. Now, he was pissed, more than I'd ever seen. It always amazed me how gentle some people could seem at first though dark clouds roiled just underneath their surface. He kept the door ajar wide enough that it pinned me against the escape door, not allowing me to access it.

"Give me that stool," he ordered Lovely.

I couldn't see her, but she must've handed him whatever he'd asked for, because suddenly, he wedged a wooden counter stool into the pantry, and any pressure I put onto the stool locked it even more firmly into place. I was stuck—couldn't open the escape door, couldn't step out of the pantry without someone's help.

With one eye in the pantry and one peering around the side of the door, I watched Dr. Rivera step back and let out a heavy breath, pushing his hands through his head of gray hair. Now that he had a moment to catch his breath, he reached out, nabbed Lovely by the edge of her skirt, and reeled her in like the catch of the day.

She fought against him, still without words, slapping her meek hands against his chest, catching him in the cheek. I knew right then that she needed to stop resisting, because I could see the impatience all over his face, and a far worse outcome than his annoyance awaited her.

But she kept flailing. She had lost her patience, too. Maybe years of frustration all built up inside her, but her attack grew stronger, and she drove her fist into his face, clipping him in the chin a few times before he finally plunged the kitchen knife deep into her belly.

I bit my lip.

Lovely collapsed into a heap spilling wider per second with dark red blood.

"Why?" I cried, resting my head against the door frame. I sobbed at the insanity of it all. How had it all degenerated so quickly? "Why did you do that? She didn't do anything to you. You're the monster."

I should've remained quiet, but there was nothing to lose at this point. It was just me and the doctor, and I was pretty sure I was done hiding from him. My fate now rested in his mercy and any ability I had left to sneak my way out of this.

"She betrayed me, *niña*. Or wasn't that clear?" He wiped his lip of blood from the cut Lovely had given him.

"She was scared of you."

"She was a child, she didn't listen," he spat like a father defending his violent disciplinary actions against his family.

I wasn't going to argue the obvious—that Lovely had been a middle-aged woman, not a child. But if he could think of his wife's corpse as a pseudo-living thing and his art studio as a place to reanimate her, his delusions were the least of my problems.

"You should've told your husband to come get you," he snickered, shaking his head in amazement. "But you women now, you feel like you don't need anybody, not even the men here to protect you."

I wanted to spit in his face for suggesting anything about my gender when he had no idea what it was like living as a woman in this world, but a part of me knew he was right. I *should've* told Samuel to come home to Miami, to call the police. Why hadn't I listened to my instinct? Why insist that everything was fine?

Why put my need to prove myself above my own safety?

Now, I was stuck inside a freaking pantry while the old man who'd lured me here searched through drawers in a cabinet for what, I had no idea. But he kept talking about young women, how they'd changed from when he was a young man, how they'd gotten stupider with time.

I ignored him. If I could somehow twist my hips, I might be able to angle them in such a way to climb over this stool. But then I'd have to run past the doctor and try every door as he chased me. No matter what, I was screwed, unless I leaped from a window.

"So, now you know about my secret room. My cellar that's not a cellar," he said, pulling something out of a drawer and holding it up in the darkness. A ball of string or twine or something. He came over and fumbled with it, using the knife to cut himself a length. "Don't judge me, *niña*. I gave those girls a good life before I expired them. It's no different than your generation taking in stray dogs or cats."

"Except we don't kill our dogs and cats after we rescue them," I said. Maybe there was something in the pantry I could use to disarm him, but all there was were cans of spaghetti sauce and boxes of pasta.

Dr. Rivera's tone was flippant. "Eh, I guess you're right. But your generation is way too compassionate. The more you care about others, the less you care for yourself. That's why you're in this predicament to begin with. Your compassion makes you weak."

"Screw you. It beats being a psychopath with no regard for life like you."

He regarded me with a raised eyebrow. "You think so?" He chuckled. "I rather thought of myself as a charming caregiver. I helped quite a number of patients in my time, *señorita*. Cured many."

Reaching into the pantry, he gripped one of my wrists and pulled it toward him. I winced, as he nearly broke my elbow. Resisting him only threatened to break my forearm, so I let him wrap the length of twine around my wrist while I stared at the pantry. Grabbing the first thing I could—a glass jar of pickles—I hurled it backwards hoping to smash his forehead with it, but he swerved in time and the jar broke on his tile floor.

"Look, why don't you stop resisting. Just let me do this and get what I need from you, and maybe I'll let you go. I promise."

He lied, and I knew it. I had no chance to do anything from this position, and at least he was looking to tie me up, not reach into the pantry with his knife and slice me up. He was strong for an older man. He found my other wrist and tied the two together so hard, I lost feeling in both hands. Yanking back the stool, he fished me out of the pantry.

Stumbling out, nearly slipping on the pool of Lovely's blood, I had no choice but to let him lead me through the house, hands bound behind my back. He pushed me through the front door into the darkest night and around the house.

The warmth of the outside air might've been the last I'd ever feel.

Swinging me around the side of the house, he reached a door opposite the garage, unlocked it with a key from his pocket, and pushed me inside. The room was musty and dark, but he flipped on a switch and showed me down a ramp that twisted a couple of times before he pushed open a heavy wooden door, and we were back where we started this chase.

Inside the cellar.

I could've made a crack about the cellar being real after he said it didn't exist, but he still held the knife in his other hand, and I didn't want to suffer Lovely's same fate. From this side of the room, I saw many things I hadn't from the tunnel side.

Mrs. Rivera's corpse, for one. Up close and personal. From this angle, I could tell she was definitely dead, a hard, drying body that'd been spectacularly painted using elements of trompe l'oeil with highlights and shading to look hyper-real. Her eyes were fake, though. Two, glistening real-looking orbs like small billiard balls with purple irises.

Purple irises.

Bibi's port wine stain.

A holding cell, for two. It looked almost exactly like the one in the Pirates of the Caribbean ride at Disney, complete with iron bars and a padlock, and I knew in a heartbeat that he was about to throw me in there before he did, and the door clanged shut, catching my ankle in the process. I screamed, because of how much I hated him.

And the pale dress ghost, for three.

Standing behind him.

TWENTY-TWO

My foot burned with pain. *Damn it.*

Why did he have to slam the door on me before I was all the way in? Now I was in a cage and hurt. In a freakin' cage. A thought of Samuel came to mind asking if I was all right, if I needed him to come home. I'd said no, I was fine.

Damn it, damn it.

Why?

Why had I insisted to be fine?

I'd been taught that we were all born with intuition, a mild form of sixth sense. That we were all psychic to a certain degree. I knew everything wasn't okay, yet I'd pretended it was, so Samuel wouldn't worry. What good was intuition if I habitually ignored it? What good was keeping peace if it led to chaos?

The ghost in the pale blue dress had floated all the way up to the cage bars. Curiously, she looked inside at me, regarding me like a trapped animal or a puzzle for her to solve.

I kicked at the solid bars. There was little chance of getting out of here, and the truth of that hit me hard. Random objects littered the cage—a hair tie, a shirt button, a sock—and the space smelled of urine.

Great.

I was going to die in here.

And my family would discuss how naïve I'd been to come to this house alone. In the end, my stubbornness had been my downfall. My need to feel special. I sobbed against the bars, pressing my forehead into them, letting the tears come. My only consolation…that I'd managed to get Bibi out. Through her survival, this torture would mean something.

But now, all of Samuel's and my hopes and dreams of one day starting a family, of growing old together, would never come. Samuel would mourn my death then move on, find someone else to love. Someone reserved, timid, with less sense of adventure. Someone who'd survive Life and not leave him wifeless.

I literally ruined everything.

The ghostly woman left the cage, reappearing on the opposite wall of the art studio. She looked helpless, like she didn't know what to do anymore to stop the insanity.

The doctor felt her presence. He shivered in the cold and muttered, "They won't leave me alone."

I wouldn't either if I was dead. I'd haunt him until his head exploded, until his brain melted from trying to figure out the "science" behind the haunting, and now I understood the pale dress ghost's motive.

From my cage, I had a clear view of it all—of the demented flesh painting, the doctor pacing the studio putting things in place. He needed order, or lose his mind. The doctor suffered some sort of overt obsessive compulsive disorder. And Barbara Rivera's corpse sitting in her wheelchair, staring into nothingness. A corpse. The doctor thought of his wife's corpse as real.

I shifted my stare to the painting's violet eyes and saw how they matched the corpse's fake ones. "Did you make those with my friend's…" I couldn't finish the question. It was hard enough imagining what he'd done to Bibi to get that patch of skin.

He glanced at the artwork then at me. "Her port wine stain? Yes, you like it?"

"You're sick, you know that?"

"I see how you think of me, but consider that I let her live, since I only needed her facial skin. Other subjects weren't as fortunate."

"Why not?" A tremor slipped into my voice.

He picked up a scalpel and ran his fingers along the blade. "Every part of this painting was made with corresponding parts of the body. The arms were made with skin from the arms, the legs were made from skin with the legs. Except for the eyes and hair, of course, since I decided to go with a unified crepe look."

I was flabbergasted. I kept imagining what he did to other women to get the "unified crepe look" that he wanted.

He stepped up to the painting and touched it gingerly, lovingly. "My wife started it while pregnant and never got to finish it. I've done my best to keep her vision going, but I'm not half the artist she used to be."

"I doubt her vision was to use skin."

"No, that was my addition, but it does give a unique texture, *verdad*? Almost like it was scraped together with oils using a spatula. I love it." He touched the pregnant belly, mostly empty except for the original painting underneath. "I thought you could go right here."

Me?

He planned to use my skin. "You say I'm pregnant, but you could just be saying that for your own purposes."

"I assure you I'm not. Julia Harding has never been wrong. Why do you think I bought this house?"

So he could seek out pregnant victims? He was mad as hell.

"All this, and this…" He pointed out huge sections of the subject's pregnant belly. "All pregnant skin."

Pregnant skin? He was talking like they'd been objects instead of victims. I held back a sob. "I'm not going to be a part of your painting, Dr. Rivera."

"Oh, but you are. I waited so long for pregnant skin to come along so I could use it for my beloved's *barriga*."

"I'm not 'pregnant skin.' I'm a person. My name is Queylin, and I'm not part of your twisted art project."

"You'll feel differently when you realize a part of you will live forever this way."

I didn't want to live forever. I wanted to live temporarily, freely, happily with my family and friends, not forever in the cellar of this crazy man's malevolent home.

He pulled out a small vial of clear liquid and a syringe and I knew that injection was meant for me. Behind him, the pale dress ghost stood by his ear, screaming without making a sound. Her mouth formed an O, and as she shouted at him, veins burst from her forehead. Her thin arms swiped away tools from his table.

One vial flew across the room and landed against the brick wall, smashing into pieces.

"See?" He sighed, shaking his head. "This is why I hired you. They don't leave me alone. They torment me, even though they can travel anywhere in the cosmos, but no, they stay here to taunt me."

"Because you ruined their lives. They want you to pay," I said.

"I won't pay. I live alone. Nobody bothers me, and nobody gets out once they know what I do here." He cast me a quick smile.

I swallowed.

"My friend did."

The smile on his face dissipated. "Yes. And whose fault is that? I already took care of Lovely. Now you."

The jab reminded me that there was still hope for me. By now, Bibi might've reached civilization and alerted the police. Then again, she was so weak when she left, she might've hit pavement unconscious or be out in the garden somewhere, face first in a ditch.

"God willing, none of that will happen."

"For someone who doesn't believe in God, you talk a lot about Him," he said, preparing another injection then wiping his hands on a paper towel.

"I never said I don't believe in God," I said. "I don't believe in organized religion. I pray my own way, but I do believe in a higher power."

"Yes? Well, you're going to need Him. Let's see if He appears for you. Lord knows, he didn't appear for me. He took my wife. He took my child…"

It wasn't your child, I thought.

"I can make her live again," he said, turning to the painting. He nodded, proud of his work.

"You can't play God," I told him. "Nothing will ever bring her back, not even what you're doing here. You know that, right?"

"I'm cursed, Quey*lín.* Cursed by *La Dama de Blanco.*"

"I thought you didn't believe in curses." Two could play this game.

"Touché, but we shall see. So far, the curse lives on. No children, no babies, no viable pregnancies."

"Coincidences," I said.

Now I was being the rational one. I didn't believe Julia Harding had actually cursed this house. I thought her legacy had prevented good things from happening

188

over the years, but that was to be expected from a home filled with so much negative energy.

Something buzzed in the doctor's pocket. He pulled out a phone—*my* phone. "Oh, I have this, by the way. You left it alone in the room."

"Let me have it."

"You're in no position to make demands of me, young lady." He laughed. "Besides, I've been answering your texts for you."

"What? No. Give it to me."

"Your husband asked if you were okay. I told him you were fine and didn't need any help. You know, because that is how you women are now. You demand knights in shining armor, then when you get them, you demand they give you space to conduct your own lives."

"That's not true."

"You want to know why I preserve my wife's body? Because she was one of the last true women. She knew her place and she respected mine."

"She was a prisoner," I said. "Who suffered from Stockholm Syndrome. Even now, she's scared of you. I would hardly call that respect."

"What do you mean *even now*?" His dark eyes flickered at me, eyebrows drawn into the center of his forehead.

Wait, he didn't know? That his wife haunted this house? That all he had to do was reach out to her and she might come to him? I had to use this amazing new revelation to my advantage somehow.

"Your wife is here."

"What do you mean? Who told you that?"

"Your wife did."

"But my wife is here." He gestured to the wheelchair.

I couldn't with this man. "Her ghost lives in your guest bedroom. Or didn't you know? Oops, I guess you

189

shouldn't have set me up in there. Her spirit haunts this house, Dr. Rivera. I've seen her. I've seen her many times."

He flew to the cage, fingers gripping the iron bars. "Why do you say this?"

"Because it's true."

"What does she look like?"

"Like that painting, only more beautiful. With bright violet eyes. But she's in deep emotional pain."

"Why in pain?" His eyes filled with tears, and for a second, I actually felt sorry for him.

"Because she hates what you are doing. She hates that you torture and kill people." I didn't know if she did or didn't, but it couldn't hurt to say it.

"But I am doing it for you, *querida*," he begged the air, his eyes turning pink with tears. Before my eyes, the doctor's stony expression turned to heartbreak. "I do it so you can live again!" He broke down and sobbed, his fluffy white hair shaking against the iron bars.

I might've reached out to grab him had my hands not been tied behind my back.

I closed my eyes and went with my intuition. "She says to take the rope off my wrist."

He cleared his nose with the back of his hand. "She would not say that."

"Yes, she wants to take possession of me. She wants to use my hands."

"For?"

"So she can caress your face. She misses you. I won't escape, doctor. I'm in a cage, for shit's sake."

He thought about it for a split second. He lifted his tear-stained face to gauge mine. I almost felt bad lying to him. Almost.

"Turn around." He sniffled, standing to grab something off his table. I turned around, pressing my tied hands against the iron bars. Using one of his tools, he carved at the restraints until my wrists broke free.

"Now come back the way you were," I instructed. "She wants so much to hold you again."

Behind him, the pale dress ghost laughed.

Pressing his forehead to the bars, he resumed his sobbing. "I'm sorry, *querida*. I'm sorry to disappoint you. *Como te extraño, querida. Por favor, discúlpame.*" He begged for his wife's forgiveness and waited to feel her touch, the touch I was about to give him.

Reaching out slowly, I slid my fingers into his thick, white hair. The moment I did, he broke down even more, crying against the bars.

My heart pounded so hard, I thought he might detect it in the stillness. I wished this moment could've been different. I wished I could've actually delivered a tender message from beyond the grave for this mourning man.

But I couldn't.

I had to live.

Grabbing fistfuls of his hair, I yanked him against the iron bars with every ounce of force I had, slamming his forehead into the metal. I did it again and again, smashing him several times, as his hands tried to wrench mine free, but I wouldn't let go, not even as he used the scalpel in his hand to swipe at my hands over and over.

I would not let go.

Finally, he fell onto his side, knocking into his table, his pans and cups and vials and tools of torture all come crashing onto the floor, rolling every which way. Reaching out between the bars, I tried to get the one item I needed—the key—from the old man's pocket, but I couldn't extend far enough.

"Come on…" I muttered, gritting my teeth.

The pale dress ghost, watching my struggle from the ceiling, dove toward me, used what little energy she had left to hoist the old man onto his side. Then, the key slipped out of his pocket and onto the hard stone floor.

I reached for it again, bruising my armpit in the process. Just another inch and I would be able to reel it in with my fingertips, but I didn't need to. The pale dress ghost rolled in like a soft fog, nudged the key the last inch toward me, and quietly disappeared from this world.

TWENTY-THREE

I had only a moment.

The old man was moving, albeit slowly while muttering nonsensical things. From the blood loss, I thought he'd be passed out a while, but now I wasn't sure.

Taking advantage, I took the key and pressed it into the lock, giving it a twist, which was hard to do from the angle behind the bars, but the lock popped open, and I pushed my way out of the holding cell.

The iron bars pressed against Dr. Rivera's side, and I thought he would awaken from the pressure, so the first thing I did was grab my phone. For some reason, I felt compelled to pause and stare at Barbara's dehydrated mummified body one more time. I felt her sadness and desire to end the pain.

I wished the ghostly Barbara, wherever she was in the house or the ether, a peaceful passing into the other life. *I'm sorry for everything that happened to you,* I thought.

Wedging my way past the doctor, careful not to step on him or brush any part of his body with my feet, I stepped quietly all the way to the door, pushed down on the crank, and entered the outside world. It was still dark, though early morning, and I could feel the energy of the sun ready to rise over the horizon.

There was something about this time of day that always unsettled me. It was when I'd lie beside my husband having my craziest dreams, when the veil between the worlds felt the thinnest, when I'd often see shadows shifting up and down the walls.

I'd never experienced true magic until I stood beside Harding Estate at six in the morning, staring at the deep orange tones of the horizon, facing the guardians of the east, watchtower of air, facing the great Mother Ocean, knowing I'd just escaped the worst situation of my life. That full breath of air that came with freedom.

I tucked behind a coquina wall and fumbled with my phone. In stressful dreams, I often couldn't punch numbers, press buttons, or remember simple things like 911. But I breathed deeply, remembering to stay calm and texted Samuel first, knowing if I made an actual call or spoke aloud, the old man might hear me.

Not okay. Need help. Police.

Thank heavens autocorrect was on, or none of the words I texted with shaky hands would've come out right.

WHERE RU?

Samuel was both pissed and worried. I hoped he would some day forgive me.

Harding Estate, I replied, but autocorrect did not recognize my trembling message, so I tried again... *Send help ASAP—*

I couldn't send it. My phone was suddenly yanked from my hand, and the doctor, agile and persistent as he was, smashed it against the rough crushed shell exterior of the house. Glass pieces crumbled to the ground.

"You're not leaving," he panted, mouth gasping for air. In his right hand was the fucking syringe.

"You're not making me stay." My gaze burned at him.

He still managed to chuckle under his breath. "You're so confident. Your generation sure is determined…if tremendously foolish."

I wasn't going to insult his generation in return. They had raised my parents, who, in turn, had raised me, so if anyone was responsible for the way we horrible millennials had turned out, it'd be his.

I stared at him, urging my brain to think of a way out of this.

"I need you in order to complete the painting," he said blankly, as if such a thing were even an option.

I had to remember that this man was totally insane, that he didn't think rationally like regular people. In his mind, he probably thought I would be fine with sacrificing my skin for the pregnant belly of his fucked-up skin art.

"It's not going to happen, doctor. And I already alerted my husband. The police will be here soon. You may as well give up."

Inject yourself, you piece of shit.

"No. No, no, no." Wearing an odd expression of disbelief and amusement, he encroached on me slowly across the back patio. I stepped backwards and tripped on every rocking chair along the way. There was only one thing to do at this point—outrun him.

I turned and ran.

He chased me.

The old man chased me.

We were only as old as we felt. The asshole caught up with me and twisted the hell out of my arm. I screamed, fairly sure he had broken something. His syringe brushed against the crook of my elbow, but there was no way I would let him fill me with chemicals or any of his wicked ideas.

I kicked him hard, causing him to fall backwards against a rocking chair. He stumbled, and I set off running again, but he reached out, pulled on my shirt, and brought me to the ground. I slammed my head against one of the wooden columns of the back porch and for a moment, all I saw was blackness and stars that exploded into a radiating pattern.

Stars.

And blackness.

Coming to, I saw that my leg was being pulled by my ankle by a strong hand. My shirt had slid up along my upper back, my whole bra and stomach was exposed, as the old man dragged me along the patio floorboards back toward the side of the house with the cellar door. Even without seeing them, I knew my back was full of bloody scratches.

As he dragged me off the porch, however, I reached out to the last object I could get my hands on—a last flailing attempt—and caught a wide wooden coffee table between two rocking chairs. My nails scratched and I nabbed one leg and took the damn thing with me. As the doctor tried to drag me off the porch, the table wedged between the columns, stopping his efforts.

He turned, annoyed to see what was causing him so much trouble, and the next thing he saw was a flying rocking chair coming straight at him. I'd stood and grabbed the nearest one, and while I never thought I'd ever be strong enough to lift a rocking chair above my head, adrenaline was an amazing thing.

So was the will to survive.

So was the human brain.

And so I hoisted that chair over my head and whirled it through the air straight at him. He tried blocking his face with it, but it clocked him in the temple, and a gash opened up, releasing a thin line of blood seeping into his eyes.

"*Coño! Me cago en...*" he cried out.

Though I'd little energy left, I found the last of my reserves and ran. Ran as fast as I could across the back patio, coming out the other end and tripping to the ground right at the angel statue's feet.

"Shit."

I scrambled to my feet again, and the lantern turned on, glowing brightly in the early morning hours, but the doctor came running around the side of the house and tackled me like a linebacker. Together, we stumbled and hit Julia Harding's tombstone, tumbling into the tall grass.

I wasn't sure how I knew this, but Julia was here now, watching us struggle, and the old man's hard grip wrenched my waist, as another hand slipped around my neck. His fingers dug into my throat, I saw the syringe come up over his head, and watched it come down, almost in slow motion, toward my neck.

His arm, so close to my cheek, was in the perfect position for me to swivel my face and sink my teeth deep into his wrist. As he screamed out, letting go of the syringe, it flew into the grass, and I tasted blood and hated it, hoped to God and the Universe that I wouldn't catch something from this foul man's life essence. He let go, brought his hand to his chest, and cradled his wounds.

"*Puta*," he spat, eyes filled with hate.

Ah, yes, *puta*. Bitch. Whore. The word women the world over had to endure through centuries of humiliation anytime they dared to defend themselves. I owned that word with full pride.

"Your own fault, asshole."

And then he flew down on me again. I had no time to roll out of the way, and a split second later, I felt the pressure of his entire weight on my body, crushing me. Ribs cracked and internal organs buckled under his weight, but I kept my core muscles tight to fend him off as long as I could.

Full of anger, he struck my face with his fist, over and over, then twisted his hands around my neck and began choking me. I nearly blacked out again. I was pretty sure this was it. I could only muster up enough energy, and my muscles were officially giving out. My weaker body mass was no match for his larger one, and this position left very little for wits or defense strategy to accomplish.

Worse, with my head twisted to one side, I had a direct view of Lovely, dead against the inside French door. His faithful servant, simply wasted. That woman had risked it all so Bibi and I could escape, could survive. Maybe deep inside, she knew she'd never be able to leave even with the doors wide open.

Some women made no attempts to leave their shitty situations, and I could only surmise that a crushed spirit had to do with that.

Well, this crushed spirit had given of herself selflessly, and I was only sorry that I never got to thank her. Flitting in and out of consciousness, as the doctor unleashed his rage on me through fist pounds and punches to the chest, I imagined myself joining Lovely in another world.

Maybe it was better this way.

Maybe my unborn child and I would find Julia and her unborn child, and this way, I might escort her to the Light. Maybe I'd already completed my job on this earth, same way Lovely had, and now my time here was done. I only wished I'd had the chance to say goodbye.

My vision turned black.

In my mind, I fought back. I punched the old man, pushed him with newfound force, and found victory in Julia's garden. I imagined the French doors opening, Lovely standing on her own feet, and reaching for her summoning stick.

In my mind's eye, she struck the end against the ground while uttering a prayer in Creole, all while the ghost of Julia Harding knelt by my head and cried over me.

But it was all in my mind.

In this dream state between life and death.

In the ashen area between worlds.

But then, why, when I opened my eyes slightly to see how bad reality was, how close to dying I might actually be, did I catch a glimpse of Lovely, eyes rolled back into her head, white glowing orbs of fierce anger and determination in the middle of her face, holding her mighty wand?

She stood at the open French doors, fingers gripped around her summoning stick.

Striking the ground with it.

Over.

And over.

And when she was done, he stood next to us, and Dr. Rivera saw him too, stopped beating me to death to stare at him, even fell back onto his hands. Roger, looking down at his beloved Julia still cradling my head, lifted a foot above the old man's chest and stepped his ghostly self right into the doctor's body.

TWENTY-FOUR

Roger, or the doctor possessed by Roger—I wasn't sure anymore—wrenched himself off me, struggling to his feet. I gasped for breath, wavering in and out of consciousness, as oxygen found its way back into my lungs. A prickling spread through my skin, tickling my throat.

Running his hand through his hair, the doctor, with Roger standing inside of his body, looked nervously to the ocean.

"They're coming," said a voice full of watery reverberation. It was the doctor who spoke, but his voice sounded different, a composite of two or more voices, none of which belonged to him.

"Who is?" I asked.

"Coast Guard." He pulled something out of his pocket, but nothing was in his hand. "Nine o'clock. I need to get past Bimini and the Rum Line before they find me. Julia...love...I have to leave, but I'll be return soon."

Julia.

I'd forgotten she was behind me. I craned my neck to find her and saw her still kneeling and crying on the ground. Could she not see Roger? She wouldn't look up or acknowledge him.

"Julia…" Roger called to her.

Julia, I tried to speak but no sound came out. *He's here. He's waiting for you.* Did they exist on separate dimensions?

I couldn't move. All I could do was lay here and feel everyone's pain at once. They say that empaths become drained of energy after absorbing emotions of those around them. Well, I absorbed Julia's—her tormented soul waiting for her lover, wondering if she would ever see him again, torn over how on Earth she would survive the next year, if she could deliver this child at all, if she would survive an attack from her husband or the community once they saw…

Once they knew.

But I also felt Roger's anguish over the Coast Guard's pursuit, how he hadn't meant to fall into this line of work, but recent laws had created the perfect storm for making a fortune illegally. How else was a boat captain supposed to make a living? He never should have laid a hand on Julia, but she was the only one who understood him. A kind, loving woman. Yes, she belonged to another man, but that man did not appreciate what he had on his hands.

Some possessed diamonds but only saw sand.

I even felt the doctor's emotions—confusion, fear of death, isolation, misunderstanding, hatred, and revenge. In this dreamlike, trancelike state, the sentiments all swirled around me, through me. They used me as a conduit, the way I'd always asked for.

Now I understood when psychics hated that I called them talented, never understood why I envied them. Who would want this? Who would want to be bombarded day and night with the energy of others? I wanted to shake off the thoughts, rip my head off, end the voices.

Scrambling to my feet, I stood looking at the angel statue, flipping and flipping my lucky bracelet. They stared back at me, solemnly communicating all the sadness they'd seen over the century. The lantern dimmed to nothing then glowed again, its power dying.

Was I dying?

Was this death?

My ability to discern between life and death, dreams or reality was growing increasingly harder. In the distance, the great banyan tree awaited me, its branches etching sharp thorns into early morning sky, puncturing layers of rose and tangerine clouds. The tree could help me end things, it seemed to communicate. All I had to do was press my bare feet into its massive roots, climb, and soon it would all be over.

The sadness would end.

I'd loved this tree for so long. But I'd only seen it at night during the urban exploration of my teen years. In the morning, it was even more beautiful, a different animal altogether. I had to see it up close, even at the risk of watching Julia hang there again.

I stepped past the statue, aware that Roger was following me. Roger always followed me. Roger understood me like no other, but the Coast Guard captain told me...he told me they'd shot him point blank. He would never be coming back for me. He would never seen his own child, and even if he could, how would we ever create a life together?

An impossible situation.

There was no other way to deal with it than to end it. After they'd arrest my husband, there'd be nothing left for me here in Florida. I never thought I'd miss the cold winters of New York City and the harsh ones of Ohio as much as I did right now.

Queylin, wake up.

Julia—they were Julia's thoughts, yet they were mine also.

I felt as though I'd lived them myself. Maybe I had. All I knew was that I had to climb this tree and finish things once and for all. I couldn't take the pain anymore. Reaching the tree, I pressed my hands into the thick trunk and tangled roots as the doctor or Roger followed me. I knew he wanted to prevent what I was going to do, but this was the only way.

The tree's energy was older than all of us put together. It called me home.

"Why do you follow me?" I asked Roger.

"My life is yours, Julia," he replied. "And that of the life growing inside of you."

The life growing inside of me.

If the doctor had been right, and the statue indeed detected those imbued with new life, I couldn't climb this tree, yet it continued to pull me in, lull me to eternal rest. I had to climb it—and did. All the way to its first branch high in the air, about twelve feet off the ground, where Julia had once taken her life and was about to take it again.

Through me.

Because time was not linear as we thought it was, and never had been. Our souls could choose any time period we wanted to be in, live inside of any body, because souls were energy, and energy could not be created nor destroyed. So, our spirits repeated moments like these, over and over, until we freed ourselves and moved on.

Julia never freed herself.

Maybe I could help her.

Now that Roger was here, maybe he could help her too. Unable to rip myself out of this reverie, I climbed across the giant branch like I had this morning, or yesterday in Queylin-time, and reached the hanging roots that made this banyan look like a prisoner of its own misery.

The doctor followed me.

Though he was old, he was fit and pressed his shoes into the roots, bobbled a little unsteadily, but rose into the tree nonetheless. He followed me along the branch. If I were to snap out of the trance and remember that I was Queylin Sanchez-Gold and nobody else, now would be the time to panic. Last thing I needed was to become uber-aware that the murderer who'd chased me all night and disfigured my friend, was now in the tree with me. I tried to keep calm and tune into Julia's thoughts instead.

No death by doctor.

I'd rather take death by choice.

Any moment now, dawn would break on a new day, and I'd be gone from this world. I'd be reunited with Roger, once and for all, and we might be happy in Heaven if I didn't become stuck in this miserable half-existence.

"Come back here." It was the doctor's voice, snapping me back to reality. "I need to finish the painting, Quey*lin*. You must do this for me."

I must do nothing, old man.

I looked down. There was no way out of this situation except by dropping from the banyan, and the ropes were already in my hands. I looked down at a tangle I'd created—a noose. I had to fulfill this destiny and place it around my neck. I never quite belonged in this world anyway.

Were they my thoughts?

Or Julia's?

It all blended into one. I'd never suffered serious depression. This was how it felt.

I shook my head, trying to pry the evil thoughts from my mind. "Get it together, Queylin. Snap the hell out of it. Come on…"

In the distance, I heard sirens wail. The police had been alerted. Bibi had reached the highway. I could jump to the ground and run to them, break several bones, but at least I'd be alive. Leave Dr. Rivera up in this tree for the police to find, and it would've been a fine decision had I not been so trapped in this otherworldly pull.

Julia's energy overwhelmed me, tugged at my will. Of course it did—she was filled with pain and bringing everybody down with it. That was her curse—her legacy.

Around my bare feet, I watched white wisps of fabric blow around in the breeze. I saw the thin line of blood seeping into my toes. The Lady in White—*La Dama de Blanco*—was me, inside of me, using me. She'd haunt this house and garden forever. She'd look for a way out, trapped in this lonely existence. She'd use however many warm bodies she could until she found Roger.

"Julia, he's here. Don't you see him?" I begged. "Roger is there, coming at us." If she could only see him, she wouldn't need me anymore, she could go with him into the Light, and I'd finally be released from this trance.

"Roger?" I spoke through a different voice. "Roger, I'm coming to you, my love."

For a moment, I thought she might snap out of it, but I could hear what was in her mind clear as a bell. She'd been abandoned. By another man. Again. She could not redeem this life, so she would escape it and start all over in a new one.

"It doesn't have to be this way," I told her. "Julia, go towards the light. You're already free," I tried explaining again.

She listened, holding the banyan's roots limply in her hands. My hands. We were one and the same now. I touched my bracelet, imagined its power emanating and surrounding us with love. With light. Of course I believed in God, because we *were* God, created in His image. We all held the power to create our own destinies, exactly like Him.

This was not my fate. It couldn't be.

The sirens approached, just as Dr. Rivera inched toward me, reaching for me and side-stepping to avoid losing his balance. "Julia, don't. Don't jump," he said in Roger's voice. Julia's lover's features were superimposed over the doctor's.

Handsome.

Worrisome.

I wanted this nightmare to end, this inability to control my own body and mind. My rational side told me to throw this noose over Dr. Rivera's head and let gravity decide his fate, but I knew I couldn't do that. Even after all that had happened, I couldn't kill a man.

"Julia, stop!" Roger cried out.

She paused, looked at Roger/Dr. Rivera, our eyes connecting for the first time since Roger appeared. Finally, she saw him. I knew because I suddenly felt my heart ache turn to beating recognition and elation.

He came for me, after all.

I threw my arms out to reach for him—Julia reaching for Roger, yes—but also Queylin reaching for the man who wanted to kill her, nearly losing my balance in the first place. But I stopped and pulled back.

No, I couldn't.

"I'm sorry, Julia, but I can't let you take us both down," I said. If I was pregnant, which I was, I knew I was—I could feel the fluttery sensations inside of me. "I'll name my baby after Roger," I told her.

I would help them both live on in some way, but I couldn't take this fall.

That would be lovely.

She smiled. Julia Harding smiled, lifting my heart which smiled for her in return. I felt her pure happiness at my words, but I didn't have time to fully enjoy them, because Dr. Rivera reached me on the tree limb, grabbed me by the shoulders, and tugged on me to make me fall.

Which I did.

But I held on at the last moment, stomach rubbing against rough branches, my legs dangling below me. At that moment, Julia slipped from my body and fell into Roger's arms, taking the noose with her. Together, the three of them plummeted off the limb. I turned my face, wincing to avoid it. But I heard it loud, clear—the crack of Dr. Rivera's neck punctuating the morning stillness.

Julia and Roger evaporated from Harding Estate. The fervent glow of the angel's lantern died to a buzzing thrum before going dark altogether. And the police cars arrived.

TWENTY-FIVE

A curtain of darkness spread open, as soft fluorescent lights filtered through my lashes and silhouettes of multiple people looked down at me.

I'd been dreaming again.

I closed my mouth and rehydrated my lips.

The dreams were always about wine bottles and paintings and rooms decorated with the jewelry from women who'd never made it out of the house, women extinguished before me. In some dreams, I made it out into the light, ran toward the highway, and found people, the way I'd told Bibi to do, even though Bibi never made it that far.

She'd been found passed out on the side of the road, barely alive. It hadn't been her who'd called the police. It'd been my husband who'd had the good sense to realize I always ended my sentences with periods, never dashes or semicolons. He'd left the dental conference and boarded a late night flight as soon as he could, arriving at MIA around the same time two police officers helped me down from a banyan tree.

A banyan tree I couldn't get out of my head.

In other dreams, I never made it out at all. I'd wake up in a cold sweat, screaming about the dead women surrounding me on the floor or of yelling for help from a holding cell for days at a time without anyone to hear me.

One day at a time.

One day at a time, and therapy would help me forget. But for now, I had great distractions. Like these fantastic people at my bedside. Bibi was here, half her face in a bandage, along with Rain, Lorena, and Maggie. They'd only been allowed in, four at a time to see us, and it was so nice to see Bibi smiling, even if she'd been disfigured. I loved her and loved that she was still here.

"You look good," I mumbled, trying to sit up.

"So do you." She gazed at me with her good eye, and I knew she'd forgiven me long ago. That was another nightmare—the stress of not finding Bibi in the house. In other dreams, Bibi was dead.

I reached up and dabbed my fingertip along her gauzed cheek. "Did it go well?"

"Yeah, they took the graft from my inner thigh. Doctor says I should be able to take this thing off after a few weeks."

"Amazing," I said. I still couldn't hear the word "doctor" without it conjuring up images of that monster's face again.

One of my nurses walked in, the older lady with the gray hair in a ponytail, happily greeting my visitors and hovering over my line of vision. "Good morning. How are you feeling?"

"I'm good." My back hurt, and I felt like a truck hit me, but otherwise, all was A-okay. "Better than most people."

She raised an eyebrow. "So, you're the Queylin." She eyed me with a sneaky smile.

"*The* Queylin?"

"Yes, I saw your segment on the news. I didn't realize you were the lady who found out all that stuff that went down at the Harding Estate. My goodness, you've been through a lot."

"You think?" I said, and the whole room broke into laughter. Where was my husband?

"Well," she said, cocking her head. "Pretty impressive. I bet you never want to see another ghost again in your life, though, huh?"

I sighed, watching her check my IV bag. "Actually, ghosts aren't the problem. People are."

"I hear you. I can't believe that man was living there with that poor woman, and oh, my God, a corpse in a wheelchair? You can't make that stuff up."

"Yeah, no kidding," I murmured.

Though the stories about my harrowing experience had made it onto multiple news networks, and even Oprah's offices had called to invite me to come on and talk about it when I was ready, I couldn't.

Not yet.

In fact, I didn't even want my nurse bringing it up and was hoping nobody would ever talk about it while I was trying to recover. Maggie narrowed her eyes at the nurse when she turned around, and unsurprisingly, she changed the topic.

Because Maggie equaled magic.

"Daddy's coming now. He was showing family the new addition in the nursery," she explained. "All your levels are good. I'll have them bring your lunch in now."

"Great. Thank you." I smiled.

"Queylin," Rain said, her eyes filling with tears. "She's so beautiful. Oh…my…God. Like, seriously beautiful."

My water had broken at five in the morning. By six, I'd been wheeled into an emergency C-section thanks to the staff losing the baby's heart rate, and for the longest five minutes in the world, I thought I would lose her— my sweet angel.

But she'd had what the obstetrician called a true knot, a complete, tight knot in the umbilical cord, which cut off her heart rate until they pulled her out safely. It occurred in about 2% of all births.

Luckily, they'd given me an epidural shortly before it happened, so I was ready for surgery, and they had her out in five minutes, her Apgar scores coming out at all perfect 9s. Healthiest baby ever.

Speaking of which…

A little plastic hospital bin rolled into the room decorated with pink ribbons, followed by another nurse and then my husband, all smiles. Tired but in a great mood. This event was just what we needed. A distraction in our lives.

My staff—friends, really—all *ahhed* and cooed, and Maggie was already washing her hands so she could hold the little girl. But no way on Earth would she be first. Because Lovely Julia Gold was the most beautiful baby in the world, and Mommy needed her so very much, exactly as much as she needed Daddy, and everyone else could wait.

The bin wheeled all the way up to my bedside, and I sat up through my pain, getting ready to hold her for the first time since the birth. Had it been a boy, I would've stayed true to my word and named him Roger, but when we found out I'd be having a girl, I had the privilege of naming her after the two women who'd saved my life.

My life and Bibi's. I still suffered from the guilt of involving her, something that would take years to get over, the therapist said, but we would work it out together, as Bibi had her own therapy to get through as well.

As the nurse pushed down the safety bar at my bedside, Samuel slipped his hands underneath the little burrito bundle with the pink-and-blue, standard-issue beanie and placed Lovely in my arms. She had perfect skin, so smooth and soft, her nose was turned up like a button, and her little breathing noises melted my heart.

The tears curled over my cheeks.

I couldn't stop them. Nor did I want to.

I'd cried a lot over the last six and a half months. Out of fear, out of worry, out of guilt, out of panic, out of low self-esteem, out of love and appreciation for my husband, out of many things. But this was the first time I'd cried out of pure elation. Because while everything wasn't perfect and never would be again, it sure as hell came close.

Surrounded by friends.

Kissed by Samuel.

Holding my newborn.

Brand new path, new opportunities. Lovely had it all ahead of her, and I would do all I could to make sure she stayed safe in this world. Maybe my bracelet could pass on some of that good luck and energy. Because despite all that had happened, I still thought I'd turned out blessed in the end.

Still, more blessings couldn't hurt. Opening her swaddling just a bit, I slipped the monk's lucky bracelet off my wrist, doubled it up and slipped it onto my daughter's wrist.

Brand new beginning.

Brand new life.

Just in case.

Book 1 – Haunted Florida

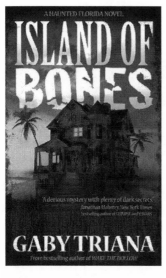

When Ellie Whitaker leaves her dead-end job and ex behind to spread her grandmother's ashes in tropical paradise, the last thing she expected was to face more ghosts of the past.

But darkness lurks inside her grandmother's former home turned resort. Ellie's presence stirs up its energies. As a hurricane creeps closer to the island, she must hurry to discover long-buried truths.

About her treasure-hunting grandfather's death in 1951. About the curse her grandmother left behind. About the innkeeper next door with an evil secret.

And the spectral visions she keeps having. Some there to help her. And some to make sure Ellie becomes a ghostly resident of haunted Key West forever.

Book 2 – Haunted Florida

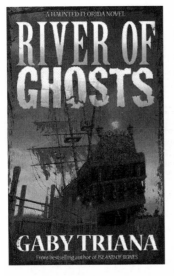

A ghostly pirate ship. A haunted cabin rotting in the swamp. Gladesmen from the Everglades' checkered past.

Avila Cypress gives airboat tours of the Everglades with a little something extra--tales of the supernatural. When a ghost adventures production crew offers her money in exchange for her guiding them to the abandoned Villegas House, a haunted depot with a murderous past in the middle of nowhere, Avila must decide if the opportunities are worth upsetting her traditional Miccosukee Indian family.

As soon as they arrive, strange things begin to happen--disembodied voices, visions of victims long gone, negative emotions. The deeper they delve into the cabin's past, the more they stir up the evil energies. Guests begin turning on each other, and Avila wonders if she made a mistake in coming. Can she develop her untapped gifts in time to save the crew from self-destruction? Or will she become another spirit to wander the River of Grass forever?

About the Author

GABY TRIANA is the bestselling author of *Island of Bones, River of Ghosts, City of Spells, Wake the Hollow, Summer of Yesterday*, and many more, as well as 40+ ghostwritten novels for best-selling authors. Gaby has published with HarperCollins, Simon & Schuster, and Entangled, won an IRA Teen Choice Award, ALA Best Paperback Award, and Hispanic Magazine's Good Reads of 2008. She writes about ghosts, haunted places, and abandoned locations. When not obsessing over Halloween, Christmas, or the paranormal, she's taking her family to Disney World, the Grand Canyon, LA, New York, or Key West. Gaby dreams of living in the forests of New England one day but for the meantime resides in sunny Miami with her boys, Michael, Noah, and Murphy, her husband Curtis, their dog, Chloe, and four cats— Daisy, Mickey Meows, Paris, and the reformed thug/shooting survivor, Bowie.

Visit Gaby at **www.GabyTriana.com** and subscribe to her **newsletter**. Also, check out her blog at: **www.WitchHaunt.com**.

Also by Gaby Triana

Horror:
ISLAND OF BONES
RIVER OF GHOSTS
CITY OF SPELLS

Paranormal Young Adult:
WAKE THE HOLLOW

Contemporary Young Adult:
CAKESPELL
SUMMER OF YESTERDAY
RIDING THE UNIVERSE
THE TEMPTRESS FOUR
CUBANITA
BACKSTAGE PASS

Author Links

Website: www.GabyTriana.com
Blog: www.WitchHaunt.com
Facebook: Gaby Triana
Instagram: @gabytriana
Twitter: @gabytriana

Made in the USA
Middletown, DE
02 July 2021

43526137R00132